UNDERWORLD

SHADOWS OF THE VOID BOOK 5

J.J. GREEN

1

S ayen was the first to notice that the shuttle they were in wasn't flying to its scheduled destination. She was sitting in a window seat and was in no mood for talking. After telling Carl what she'd found out at the Global Government Security Headquarters, their conversation had drifted to silence. She was worried about her parents. She wondered what their message meant in terms of their own safety. They'd written that it was no longer safe for her to go home, but had they meant that it was unsafe for her because the Shadows were looking for her, or that their house was under threat of attack? She had no way of finding out because they'd also told her not to do anything that would allow them to be traced, and that included contacting them.

Her thoughts had preoccupied her so much that she hadn't really been registering her view of the landscape below. When her ears popped, the sensation jolted her out of her distraction. The shuttle was descending. She scanned the ground for a familiar sight of her state's capital, and with growing alarm she realized she didn't recognize what she saw. Instead of a large metropolis, below them was a small town. On the horizon was a mountain range that she knew, but it lay in the wrong direction.

She clutched Carl's arm on the seat rest beside her.

"Something's up, isn't it?" he asked in an undertone.

"Yes," Sayen replied quietly. "We're landing in the wrong place. How did you know?"

"We started descending too soon." He leaned over her to peek out the window. "Do you know where we are?"

Sayen nodded. "At least three hours' drive from where we should be." She looked past him toward Jas and Makey across the aisle. The kid was asleep, his head lolling against the security officer's shoulder. The woman was staring at the back of the seat in front of her, her face set and expressionless.

"The pilot hasn't made an announcement," Carl said, "so he's in on it." He reached across the gap between his seat and Jas's and pulled on her sleeve.

She snapped out of her reverie. "What?" she asked him, frowning.

Sayen waved to get her attention. She pointed out the window and shook her head in an exaggerated gesture. Jas's eyebrows rose. She mouthed the word *krat* and pushed Makey upright so that he woke up. As he opened his eyes, she put her finger to her lips and leaned over to whisper in his ear.

Around them, a hum of conversation rose in the cabin as some of the passengers also began to notice the shuttle wasn't landing where it was supposed to.

A ping sounded from above as the overhead speaker came to life. "This is your pilot speaking. I'm sorry to report that bad weather has forced us to divert to Silversville. An autobus will ferry passengers on to your scheduled destination. We apologize for any inconvenience. We will be landing in fifteen minutes. Please stay seated with your seatbelt fastened."

Sayen looked at the clear blue sky outside. *Bad weather?* The rest of the passengers weren't buying the excuse either. Angry voices rose on both sides of the cabin and call buttons chirped as people demanded the attention of flight attendants. The attendants all seemed to have disappeared, however. A few men and women undid their safety belts and got up out of their seats, and the volume of protests and complaints inside the shuttle rose.

"Are y'all thinking what I'm thinking?" Sayen asked the others. They nodded. There was no need to spell it out. Shadows were in control of the plane. The only question was, was this a general kidnapping, or did the aliens know that Sayen and her rescuers were on board? There weren't many shuttle flights from Antarctica. It wouldn't have taken a genius to narrow down the possibilities as to where they were, and the news of her escape from the Shadows' base must have gotten out by now.

Jas was standing and taking down her bag from the overhead locker. After putting the bag on her seat, she said to Sayen and Carl. "We can't let them stay in control of the shuttle. If we go along with their plan, they're going to have a nice reception committee waiting for us when we land. Carl, can you fly this?"

"Probably," he replied.

"If you can get us on the ground without killing everyone, that'll be good enough. Sayen, how are your arms? Can you hold a weapon?"

Sayen's forearms were still painful from laser burns she'd received during her escape. "Yes, I can."

"Great. Short, sharp bursts, okay? If you melt a hole in the shuttle, we're all dead." Jas turned to Makey, who was craning his neck, trying to hear what she was saying. "You stay right where you are. You're just another passenger, okay?"

The kid scowled. Jas still hadn't forgiven him for not following orders when he'd taken part in Sayen's rescue. She grabbed her bag and surreptitiously pulled out a weapon for Sayen and Carl. "Let's go."

The three of them made their way to the front of the cabin, which was already blocked with angry passengers trying to find the flight attendants. The attendants all seemed to have retreated into the pilot's control room. Sayen hoped that none of them were human.

"Get back to your seats," Jas shouted. "Everyone, for your own safety, return to your seats and fasten your seat belts."

She got some attention, but not enough. Most of the passengers ignored her. "Who do you think you are?" asked a woman, shrilly. "We want answers. My husband is waiting for me at the spaceport. This diversion is unacceptable."

Jas raised her weapon and pointed it above the crowd. The woman gasped and stepped back. "She's got a gun. Oh Lord, she's got a gun." That got everyone's attention. The angry passengers melted away like overnight frost under the morning sun, and in a few moments their path to the pilot's cabin door was clear. The place was filled with the sound of seatbelts being hastily fastened.

Sayen and Jas advanced, and Carl brought up the rear, covering them against Shadows that might be among the men and women watching.

Jas raised her weapon to fire it at the lock on the door, but Sayen grabbed her arm and shook her head. The Shadows could be expecting them to do just that, and they would shoot as Jas went through the door. Jas frowned at her, puzzled. As Sayen put her ear against the wall, the woman's brow cleared and she lowered her gun.

Sayen listened with her enhanced hearing. No voices could be heard inside, which wasn't surprising as the Shadows communicated with their minds, but she could detect the sounds of movement and—if she listened very hard—breathing. She held up four fingers to Jas. The pilot and three flight attendants were inside. She dropped two fingers and pointed with the others, indicating the positions of two Shadows. Jas nodded and aimed her weapon. A faint *Oh my Lord,* repeated, came from behind.

Sayen aimed at where she estimated the pilot's head to be and prayed that she hit it and not the window. With a mutual exhaled breath she and Jas fired, then altered their aims and immediately fired again. The shuttle lurched, and Sayen fell onto a seat occupied by an obese man. The cabin door swung open and a laser beam shot out, narrowly missing Sayen but hitting the obese man in the gut. He shrieked, and screams and yells from the other passengers echoed his cries.

Jas shot again, and the Shadow that had fired fell out of the doorway, half its head missing. She'd killed it, but at least one of their shots had pierced the shuttle. Air whistled out, and the door began to slam shut but was prevented by the body of the dead Shadow. An alarm sounded and oxygen masks fell from overhead. Jas and Sayen jumped over the fallen Shadow and ran through the door to the flight deck, quickly followed by Carl. Two Shadows lay dead on the floor, and the pilot was slumped dead in his seat, a smoking hole through his back.

Another hole had been melted in the window, and Sayen fought not to be dragged toward it. She grabbed a serving tray that one of the attendants had dropped and flung it over the hole. The air pressure inside the cabin held it in place, and the whistling stopped.

Carl had already dragged the pilot out of her seat and was strapping himself in. As he adjusted the controls, the shuttle's steep descent began to slow.

"Where are we going?" he asked.

"Anywhere that isn't where they were taking us," Jas replied.

"Okay, I'll find an unihabited area outside the city."

Sayen removed the headphones and mic from the pilot and listened with one ear. "Please report on your position," said a voice. "Please respond."

"Who is this?" Sayen asked. "Who am I speaking to?"

A gasp sounded, then the headphones went dead. Her eyes met Jas's. "The Shadows are at space flight control too," she said.

The aliens' spread seemed to grow wider each time she encountered them, but the exchange with space flight control had told her one thing useful: the aliens couldn't communicate telepathically over long distances. For that, they relied on electronic comms, the same as humans.

2

———

By the time Carl landed the shuttle a few miles from the capital, the passengers were subdued and quiet. Makey had joined Sayen, Carl, and Jas in the pilot's cabin. The obese man sprawled unmoving in his seat, a large pool of blood beneath him. None of the passengers had made a move to attack, so either there were no Shadows among them, or they were remaining anonymous.

Landing a space shuttle on an area of unprepared, natural landscape didn't hurt the shuttle, but it destroyed the surrounding area. When they opened the doors, the smell of burning plants and scorched earth drifted inside. As they were trying to figure out a way to traverse the ten-meter drop to the ground unharmed, one of the passengers spoke up.

"Hey, what's going on? What's going to happen to us?"

"It's too much to explain now," Sayen answered, "but those things we killed weren't people. They're aliens called Shadows. They look exactly like us, and they're trying to take over the planet."

That drew intakes of breath and exclamations from the passengers. The *Oh my Lord* woman started up again.

"We can't help you," Sayen continued. "They're after us, and we have to get away. Maybe you can call for help, but please be very careful. The Shadows might come and pretend to rescue you, only to make you another of their victims. It'll be better if you can make your own way home. After that, tell others what happened here, but watch who you speak to. If anyone you know has disappeared for no reason for a short time, they might be a Shadow."

The passengers murmured as they digested this information. A young man stood up, and Jas instantly aimed at him. The man blanched and raised his hands. "Woah there. I just wanted to say, use the emergency slide to get down. That's what it's for."

Of course. Sayen opened the casing beside the door and activated the mechanism. A bright yellow slide inflated all the way to the ground. "Thanks," Sayen said.

"No problem. Good luck to you," replied the man, sitting down.

Jas went to retrieve her bag from her seat. The curious heads of the passengers poking out into the aisle retreated as she passed them and popped out again as she returned to the front. Sayen hoped Jas had plenty of stuff in that bag of hers to help them survive.

"Thanks for saving us, honey," piped a voice. It was *Oh my Lord*.

"Ready?" Jas asked Sayen and the others.

They jumped onto the slide one by one, and scooted out of the way immediately when they hit the bottom. The ground was still smoking from the shuttle's engines. Sayen coughed, and her eyes watered. Fifty or so meters away were some low hills. She suggested they made their way over to them as they were in the direction of the capital. She was thankful for the enhanced skin on her bare feet. In their hurry to leave Antarctica, they hadn't even stopped to buy her some shoes.

As they went along, Sayen glanced over her shoulder. The shuttle passengers were beginning to leave, sliding down to the ground. She wished them well but also feared for them. The Shadows seemed to be everywhere, surely and steadily infiltrating every avenue of life, so that soon no one would know who was their family or friend or colleague, or who was a Shadow.

In a few minutes they reached the hills and started climbing the slopes. She estimated that twelve to fourteen kilometers lay between them and the city. It was late afternoon, and if they wanted to sleep in a bed that night, they had a long walk ahead of them.

Her stomach sank as she remembered what her parents had said: *don't use anything that will allow you to be traced.* The minute they used the credchips embedded in their wrists, they would be identifiable. If they couldn't pay for anything, how were they going to stay in a hotel, or buy food? How would she buy herself some shoes? And she needed a change of clothes. Walking around in Makey's oversized loans wasn't only uncomfortable, she looked so ridiculous, she would stick out like a sore thumb.

If they were to avoid detection by the Shadows, they had to disappear, her parents had said. How they were going to do that, she didn't have the faintest idea.

As she mulled over their problems, the four of them climbed higher into the hills, following narrow tracks created by hikers. Makey led them. He seemed to have a knack for finding the quickest path through the undergrowth and often found a new track when none seemed to exist. An hour passed, then two, and still they pushed on. The sun was getting lower, and the hills stretched out before them. They were heading in the right direction, Sayen was sure, but the city remained out of sight.

"Let's rest a while," Jas said as they were passing a piece of flat, grassy ground.

They sat on the grass. Carl pulled stalk to chew and lay down, spreading out his full length on the ground. Makey sat with his back to them. He was probably still mad at Jas, or maybe she was still mad at him.

"Hey, Sayen," Carl said, "your parents said someone would meet us at the spaceport with a package. Maybe we should go there and try to find them?"

"Our flight should have landed there hours ago," Sayen said. "Do you think they'd still be waiting?"

"No," Carl replied, his face twisting with disappointment, "you're right. They'd be long gone by now."

"It wouldn't be safe for them to wait around," Jas agreed. "The Shadows will have announced that the shuttle crashed, or another excuse. They might not believe it, but there wouldn't be anything they could do. And the spaceport's so far away, we'd never make it there. I don't know what to do. I'm out of ideas."

Something had been nagging at Sayen, and then seemed a good time to bring it up. "There's one thing I can't figure out—how did y'all know where to find me? Did you find out about the Shadow base and guess I must be there?"

Carl sat up and shared a look with Jas. Neither replied to her question.

"What's wrong? Why won't you tell me?" Sayen asked.

"Sayen, I'm sorry," said Jas. "I forgot you didn't know." She pulled an interface out of her bag, brought up a screen, and handed it to her.

Sayen studied the blinking blue spot and the map surrounding it for several moments before she began to understand what Jas was telling her. "Hold on, is this me?" Her mouth fell open as the penny dropped. "My parents had me fitted with a tracer? I'm carrying a *tracer*? You've got to be kidding me." She jumped up, and Jas quickly took the interface from her. Sayen clenched her fists and looked down at her body. "Do you know where it is? Did they tell you?" She probed the skin of her stomach, hoping to feel the hard edge of a chip.

"They didn't say," Carl said. "Sayen, they were worried about you after what happened on the *Galathea*."

"I'm a grown woman, and my parents are keeping tabs on me like I'm a little girl. *Worse* than if I were a little girl. Can they even do that? It's illegal, right? It's an invasion of...*krat*. My own parents." She sat down again.

"Well," said Carl, "looking on the bright side, if they hadn't, we would never have found you. You'd still be back in the Shadow base, being experimented on."

Sayen threw him a dark look. He was right, of course, but that didn't make her feel any better. All her life her parents had been overly protective, and it had made her fearful to try new things or do anything remotely risky. She'd finally overcome that fear, only to learn her parents weren't prepared to let her go and stand on her own two feet.

"We've got to find that tracer and get it out of you," Jas said.

"Yes, we have," Sayen replied, then, suspecting that Jas's reasoning was different from hers, she added, "Why?"

"You know all about the Shadows on Earth now, and they know you do. They're trying to keep their operations secret, so they'll want to stop you from spreading the word about them. If they find out that your parents fitted you with a tracer, they'll try to use it to find you." She looked at the interface in her hands. "Come to think of it…" she said as she got up. She went over to a rock and put the interface down on it. After searching for a moment, she found another rock and brought it down heavily on the interface, shattering the plastiglass screen. Jas continued to hammer the interface until it was nothing but small fragments. Finally satisfied that the device was completely destroyed, she said, "We can't be too careful. Let's get out of here."

3

On the quarantine station in its low Earth orbit, Dr. Sparks was bored. He'd pondered the question at length, but he hadn't been able to understand exactly why Polestar insisted it had to be *him* who performed assessments on the Paths. It was true that he'd been the physician aboard the *Galathea* when it crashlanded on K.67092d, but he hadn't even seen the things before they'd been taken to quarantine.

But Polestar in its infinite wisdom had somehow connected the Paths with the only scientist on board who was well versed in the complexities of the human body, and it had ordered him to conduct tests on this new species. He could have refused, but then he would have been out of a job and without a good reference to show a new employer.

He regarded the Paths on the other side of the transparent barrier and yawned. The shapeless, fungi-like upturned bags were among the least interesting aliens he'd come across. They just sat there, not doing anything, apparently existing on nothing but ordinary air, as they didn't eat any of the variety of foods offered to them, and they didn't drink or absorb water or any other liquid.

All they seemed to do was emote. Anyone within a few meters of the creatures inevitably felt whatever the Paths themselves felt at the time. Or that was how it seemed. That was supposed to be one of the things he was investigating.

It occurred to him that maybe his boredom wasn't his, but theirs. He took several steps backward to test his suspicion. From previous tests he'd gathered that the vicinity within which the Paths had an effect on humans seemed to be limited. He left the room and went a short distance down the corridor. He was still bored.

"Sparks," said a lab tech, Rogers, approaching him, "how are you doing? Found out anything about your mushrooms yet?"

"No," intoned the doctor. "I don't suppose you have some free time? I need another human subject to test their emoting."

"Me, sit in a room with those things? You must be joking. My emotions are my own, and not to be tampered with."

"The feeling wears off almost as soon as you leave the immediate area," said Sparks. "It's completely harmless as far as I can tell."

"And it's that *as far as I can tell* that makes me repeat my response. No. Sorry." Rogers moved away. "Good luck."

He was right to be cautious, of course, Dr. Sparks mused. No one knew the long-term effects of exposure to the Paths. He hoped that wasn't something that Polestar would like him to find out. Their instructions had been annoyingly vague. He didn't think the company itself had any idea what it wanted to know, or what to do with the creatures.

Returning them to K.67092d was out of the question. Not only was the planet occupied by hostile aliens, but the Paths didn't appear to be natives of the place. No one knew where they'd come from. Sparks had scoured the Transgalactic Council databases on life forms existing and extinct, but he'd found nothing that remotely resembled them. None of the Council's experts had even been able to help with educated guesses.

Sparks wondered when Polestar would finally give up their investigations and put the strange aliens in a zoo.

He returned to his observation room. The Paths hadn't moved, but he hadn't expected them to. He sat down and brought up his latest unfinished report to Polestar on his screen. It was very short and thin on meaningful detail. He didn't think Polestar would be satisfied with it. If only he could get someone to agree to be a test subject, maybe he would find out something new. He wondered if the strength of the emotions conferred differed according to a variable within the subject.

Sparks rested his elbows on the frame around the window to the Paths' room. He steepled his fingers and gazed intently at the aliens. There had to be something else he could say. *Something.*

He blinked. For a brief fraction of a second, the Paths had seemed to change in some way, but the moment had been so short, he wasn't sure what the change had been or if his eyes had been deceiving him. He folded his arms and leaned on the window frame again. Maybe this was it. Something new that he could put in a report. He determined to not take his eyes off the aliens until the change happened again.

Sparks didn't have to wait long. After a couple of minutes, the Paths very briefly faded before returning to full visibility. He was right. They *were* doing something. He set a timer.

Two minutes and twenty-four seconds later, the creatures faded again. Sparks made a note and returned to his observation. Exactly two minutes and twenty-four seconds later, the same thing happened.

The fading seemed to be regular behavior. A fourth bout of fading supported Sparks's hypothesis. His head tilted to one side as he watched. The phenomenon was so subtle, he doubted that he would have noticed it if he hadn't been staring directly at the creatures for a sustained period of time. It occurred to him that the Paths could have been doing the same thing ever since they'd collected them on K.67092d, but no one had noticed.

He turned his attention to his screen and brought up a vid from the camera that had been filming the room that held the aliens. It took him longer than twenty minutes to detect the first fading, but once he'd seen it, the ones that followed at regular intervals were easy to spot.

Sparks smiled to himself as he brought up his report to Polestar. This new behavior he'd observed should fill it out nicely. He began to speak into his mic and his words appeared on the screen. He recorded what he'd seen directly and the corroborating evidence from the vid. He would include a copy of it with a note regarding the timing of the behavior.

As he scrolled down the report to the section on his conclusions, he paused as he wondered what to say. What did the behavior mean? Were the creatures capable of entirely disappearing? Transparent organisms weren't unusual, on Earth or elsewhere in the galaxy, but the Paths didn't seem to be turning see-through. Their entire body faded, as if they were very slightly and very momentarily *not there*. And it happened at a regular rate, almost like a heartbeat. Could it be possible that they weren't fading, but they were going somewhere? Were they able to move, but without a conventional means of locomotion, and to places not in their immediate vicinity?

Sparks gasped as another idea popped into his head. Was it possible that the Paths could move in time? Did they fade as they moved briefly into the future or the past? The most famous xenobiologists had long speculated that beings with such capabilities might exist somewhere in the galaxy, given the wealth of variety in species already discovered. Some species could do things no human had ever dreamed of.

But he must not get ahead of himself. There would be plenty of time to test his hypotheses later. He grinned. He hadn't felt this excited about practicing science since he'd been at medical school. His speculations made him feel young again.

He needed an independent verification of his observation. The fading was so difficult to spot that, even with the vid evidence, it was possible he was imagining it. He would ask a colleague to watch the Paths with him. Springing to his feet, Sparks suddenly checked himself. His elation felt odd. Was it real? Was he experiencing a genuine emotion, or was he being influenced by the Paths?

The shapeless aliens sat in their quarantine room innocently.

No, Sparks was sure their range didn't extend to the observation booth. He'd tested them on several subjects. No. He was only happy because he'd found out something interesting and was finally relieved of his terrible boredom.

He went to find Rogers.

4

It was the early hours of the morning when Sayen and the others made it to the outskirts of the city. They were still several miles' walk from downtown, where they hoped to find the kind of people who could help them in their new, cred-free lifestyle. Makey clearly couldn't go any farther that night, however. The kid was stumbling with tiredness, and Jas and Carl also looked pale and drawn.

They'd come across a stream as they descended the hills, and the water had seemed clean enough to drink. All four of them had been extremely thirsty by then and willing to take the risk. Sayen's stomach had ached with hunger for a few hours, but now she only felt a little weak for lack of food.

The suburban houses at the city's edge offered little hope of rest or sustenance. Knocking on a random door was out of the question. Whoever answered wouldn't waste much time in calling the police. Dusty and haggard from their walk, they looked like the kind of people who made suburbanites uneasy. Sayen was barefoot and wearing over-sized clothes. She was also covered in scratches and bruises from her escape from the Shadows.

"We should stop and rest up as soon as we can," she said. "We can walk the rest of the way in the morning."

"Yeah, okay," Jas replied. "If we come across a park or recreational ground, we can rest there."

It wouldn't be too hard to find such a place, Sayen knew. The residential districts of her home city were planned for convenience and for bringing up the precious children of parents who'd invested a large proportion of their income in them even before they were born.

Sure enough, halfway down the next street was a small park. Daily watering had kept the grass green during the summer heat, and shade trees provided protection from the blazing sun. Drifts of the previous year's leaves had accumulated under the hedges that surrounded a playground, and the four of them made themselves as comfortable as was possible in the circumstances. Sayen was asleep within minutes.

Not long later, it seemed, the closing of a car door awakened her. Where she was sleeping, she had a view of the road, and her heart stopped when she saw what kind of car it was. Two uniformed police officers were walking toward them.

Carl was sleeping along from her under the same hedge. She edged toward him and pushed his shoulder with her foot. He shifted but didn't wake until she pushed him again, harder. He mumbled as he woke up. The police officers heard and altered their direction, heading right for them.

Sayen was already forcing her way through the leaves and stems to the other side of the hedge, and Carl followed seconds later as he realized what was happening. Jas and Makey were on the far side of the playground. Sayen and Carl ran across to them, keeping below the height of the hedge, but the officers spotted their movement.

"Hey, wait up," called one of them.

The cop's voice woke Jas. Sayen saw her eyes snap open, and she crawled quickly over to Makey and shook him, holding a finger to her lips as he stirred.

Sayen had spotted an exit to the playground in the opposite direction from the police. She pointed toward it wordlessly.

"Hey," called the officer again, more stridently.

Now they'd been seen, there was no point in trying to hide. All four sprinted toward the exit and through it before running down a road. Sayen suspected that the police were only trying to move them on, and it seemed she was right as no shots were fired and there were no more shouts.

Sayen kept her pace slow enough for the others to keep up. They raced the length of three streets before drawing to an exhausted stop.

When the others had caught their breath, she said, "I guess a neighbor saw us and made a call."

Jas nodded. "They don't want us down and outs in their area."

"Exactly," Sayen said.

They walked slowly on through the moonlit streets, assuming the same thing would happen wherever they stopped in that upmarket neighborhood. Solar-powered streetlights cast a soft orange glow. The others were beyond tired, but they had no choice but to march on. Gradually, the houses lining the streets became smaller, and they directly abutted the road with no security fences. The houses also became older and shabbier, and more cars and autocabs drove past.

When Makey staggered and fell, they had no choice but to stop. They had wandered into an area of apartment blocks and small convenience stores. Sayen and Jas helped the kid into a large block's recessed entrance, and he lay down under the security panel. Jas sat with her knees drawn up and her head resting on her folded arms, and Carl curled in an uncomfortable-looking ball on the hard pavement. Sayen sat in a corner with her back against the apartment block door and leaned her head against the wall.

It seemed only moments later when she found herself falling backward. She managed to jerk awake just in time to prevent herself from hitting the back of her head hard on the floor. It was dawn, and the door she'd been leaning against had opened. A pair of legs in pants and heels were stepping over her, their owner cursing *good-for-nothing panhandlers*. The woman who had opened the door let go of it, so that it would have hit Sayen if she hadn't put out her hand to catch it.

She held onto the door as the woman left, not giving them a backward glance. Jas and Carl were blinking awake. Makey snored gently, his mouth hanging open.

"Hey, look," Sayen said, nodding toward the building's interior.

"We can get inside?" asked Carl. "What good's that gonna do us? Are you saying we should break into an apartment?"

"I thought about it," Sayen replied. "We could find an empty one by buzzing them all and seeing which ones don't answer, but I don't know how to get past the door security. There might be other stuff inside the building, though."

"Yeah, that's right," said Jas. "It might have a gym."

Carl looked at her like she was mad.

"Showers," she explained. "Clean water."

They woke Makey up and went inside the building. The

elevator was operated by retinal scan or voice recognition, but the fire door to the basement opened with a push, and they went down two flights of stairs. They found a gym. The equipment was sparse and old and so were the showers, but the water was hot and it was free. They had no soap or towels, but right then that didn't matter to Sayen. They all went into shower stalls.

Sayen stripped off her clothes and turned on the shower, sighing with pleasure as the warm water cascaded over her body. Her enhanced skin was already almost healed. The scratches she'd sustained in the jungle were now only slight grazes, and her bruises were light yellow. Bending over, she lifted her feet one by one and checked the undersides. They were holding up well considering the many miles she'd walked without shoes. If it hadn't been for the enhancements her parents had paid for, she could never have survived the last couple of days.

Her conscience twinged as she remembered her anger over the tracer they'd put inside her. She still thought it was wrong, but she didn't doubt their love for her.

"Sayen," came Jas's voice from beyond the shower curtain, "are you nearly done? We have to go. Someone's bound to turn up in a minute, and we can't risk another run in with the police."

"Okay," she replied as she reluctantly turned off the water. Leaning forward, she ran her hands across her head, trying to wipe away as much water as she could. She reached up to the basket that held her clothes. Wrinkling her nose, she put on the dirty underwear and clothes, tugging them over her wet skin.

They went up onto the first floor and outside. Air and her body's warmth quickly dried Sayen off as they went deeper into the city. The place was waking up, and they began to attract attention from passersby. The area they were in was still too affluent for them to pass unnoticed, but this was Sayen's home city, and she knew where they had to go. When they reached the oldest, dirtiest, most dangerous area, they wouldn't get any more stares. In their unkempt, hungry, desperate state, they would fit right in.

5

With no possibility of using their embedded credchips, Sayen and the others had to make a hard choice. They'd finally reached the area where the people the vidnews called 'underworlders' lived, and they stopped to discuss their next move.

Sayen knew she was less streetwise than the others, so she was content to go along with what they decided. It was clear that they would either have to steal to survive—running the risk of arrest with nothing but an implausible story to tell in their defense—or sell the only assets they had: the contents of the bag Jas had carried all the way from the shuttle.

The decision didn't take long to make. They decided to keep Jas's two weapons and Carl's that he'd brought from Australia. They would sell everything else. The invisibility spray could have been very useful to them, but it was also very illegal in the way that personal weapons were not, and their risk of chance encounters with the police was high now that they were homeless. The spray, the explosives, and the rest of the bag's contents would have to be sold, but with the proceeds they could buy food and maybe somewhere to sleep while they figured out what to do about the Shadows.

They decided they would try to find a buyer as quickly as possible.

Considering that it was around midday, the street they'd stopped on was quiet. Few cars seemed to drive through the underworld zone, and the ones they saw were customized, self-driving models that didn't seem to be going anywhere in particular, but only cruised up and down the streets.

It was fortunate that the street wasn't busy with traffic, as children roamed it. Even toddlers who could barely walk had been allowed out by their parents, and they tottered around, sometimes in the care of slightly older siblings, and sometimes ignored by all. Older youths also loitered a short distance away from Sayen and the others. They were unashamedly staring at them.

The adolescents seemed to be the kind of people who might know buyers for Jas's equipment. They walked over and approached one of the group, who seemed to be the ringleader. A sycophantic female follower clung to his elbow. She bore a tattoo on her right cheek of a symbol that Sayen didn't recognize. The young man bore the same tattoo on his neck.

"You want something?" he asked.

"Yes," replied Jas, "we have some stuff to sell." When the young man's face hardened and his hand went to side, Jas continued, "Not the same stuff you sell. Do you know anyone who might be interested in buying some military supplies?"

His hand left his side, and his expression relaxed. "No, I don't," he said, but his gaze fell to the bag Jas carried.

"You sure, mate?" Carl asked. "If you do know someone, they might be disappointed not to see what we've got. What if we were to go over to the next neighborhood and do our business there? Whoever's in charge round here won't like it if the opposition get hold of what's in that bag."

The girl clinging to the ringleader hooded her eyes. as she looked up into the face of her idol. She was about fourteen years old, Sayen guessed, though her face was heavily made up. The artificial coloring looked like crayon on her youthful skin. Sayen mused that she'd been learning to speak French and play badminton when she was fourteen.

The ringleader made up his mind. He shrugged and turned away. Picking up the girl under her arms, he lifted her to his lips. She squealed in excitement as he kissed her, and the rest of the gang laughed.

When it became clear that he was intent on ignoring them, Jas and the others turned and left, but they hadn't gone far before Jas spun around, her weapon out. The teenagers had followed and were right behind them. The gang rushed forward.

Beams shot out from Jas's gun, and she hit all of them but the ringleader. He was also holding a weapon, but he didn't get a chance to fire a single shot. The color drained from his face as he stared at Jas.

"I only stunned your friends," Jas said. "I don't like hurting people. But I can make an exception for you."

After a moment of internal struggle, the teenager's stare wavered, and he lowered his weapon. "I'll take you to Erielle."

He led them along the street and down a narrow alley. It was windowless, and the blank brick walls rose five or six stories high on either side. Only a few old doors broke the monotonous facade. To Sayen, it looked like something out of an antique black-and-white movie. She glanced over her shoulder to the alley entrance. The figures of the street gang were silhouettes. She hoped Jas knew what she was doing.

They arrived at a plain door covered with peeling, cracked paint. The young man knocked in a specific pattern, and the door opened. After a brief exchange with two men, they stepped out and one moved toward Jas with his hands raised, ready to pat her down.

"No," Jas said. "We're not giving up our weapons, and we're not coming inside. Your friend Erielle can come out here if she wants to do business."

"Forget it," said the man, waving dismissively. "Run away and play."

"Wait," Jas said. "I think I have something to interest you." With her free hand she reached into the bag and pulled out a device the size of her fist. "I estimate that this would take the whole building down, with your precious Erielle inside. But I'm not sure. Do you think I should find out?" She flipped open the casing with a thumb.

"Whoa, geez, lady," exclaimed the man, throwing up his hands. "We'll be back in a minute." He and the other guard went inside. The teenager who had brought them quickly left.

They waited for several minutes, until Sayen was beginning to worry that Jas really would blow the place up. But then the door opened and a woman stepped out. She was about early forties and lean, but well-defined muscles lined her arms and neck. A scar scored her cheek and ran down to her chest, and Sayen couldn't help but gasp a little at the sight of it. She rarely saw any form of physical abnormality.

She couldn't understand why the woman didn't get the scar fixed. Cosmetic surgery didn't cost a lot, and you could get it for free if you let students use you for practice.

Her sharp intake of breath had attracted Erielle's attention. Sayen fought to smooth away the expression of disgust on her face, but she wasn't fast enough. The woman had caught sight of it, and in response, she looked from Sayen's toes to her head, finishing with a gaze of pure loathing directly into her eyes.

Then the silent encounter was over, and Erielle turned her attention to Jas and the device in her hand. Her anger seemed to dissipate into mild surprise, as if she hadn't quite believed that someone was really in her alley threatening to blow the place up if she didn't come out. But Erielle was more bemused than frightened. She leaned against the alley wall, her arms folded over her chest. She was wearing baggy, dark pants and a loose tank top over bare breasts.

Still saying nothing, Erielle scrutinised each of them each in turn except for Sayen, who now merited barely a second glance. The woman had clearly made up her mind about her character. As Erielle looked at the others, Sayen could almost see the cogs of her mind turning.

"Are you interested in what we have to sell or not?" Jas asked. "We don't have all day, and we won't have trouble finding another buyer."

"You're a Martian, right?" Erielle asked. "The height and the coloring."

Jas replied, "We aren't here for small—"

"And you—you're Australian," said Erielle to Carl. "But you," she said, turning to Makey, "you, I can't place, unless—"

"Let's go," Jas said to Sayen and the others.

"Okay, okay," Erielle said. "Calm down. Come inside, and we'll talk." When Jas hesitated, she added, "You can keep your weapons."

6

———

Erielle lived in what Sayen could only describe as a 'natural' house. From the human doorkeepers to the rooms at the top of the building, it seemed to have no modern appliances. No elevator—they had to climb five floors—no interfaces on the walls, no aircon, no control panels; in fact, Sayen wasn't even sure if the place had an electricity supply until they reached their destination and she saw the lighting.

Erielle led them into a large room on the top floor. Unlike the rest of the place, the room looked relatively comfortable. A rug covered the bare boards, and worn, thick, soft floor cushions were piled here and there next to low tables. The walls looked like they'd been painted by hand, each a different bright color. Simple wooden cupboards had been decorated with intricate, multi-colored designs.

"Sit down," Erielle said, nodding toward a corner. "You look hungry. I'll get you something to eat."

They did as she invited, and she went to the door and bellowed, "Sark, food," before closing it and joining them.

She sat cross-legged opposite the group across one of the tables.

Jas was looking annoyed. "We're only here to do business. I want to know how much you'll give us for what we have. Let me show you."

"She doesn't beat around the bush, does she?" Erielle said to Carl and Makey, though for all the attention she paid Sayen, she didn't exist. When the men didn't answer her, she turned to Jas. "All right, show me."

Jas took out the contents of her bag piece by piece and placed them carefully on the table. Erielle's eyebrows rose when Jas produced the invisibility spray. The woman's carefully constructed mask of indulgent tolerance fell for a moment, and a look of excitement leaked through.

When Jas had emptied the bag, Erielle sat back. "I can't deny it. That's quite an impressive haul."

The door opened and a woman entered, pushing the door with her back as her arms were occupied with holding a large tray stacked with dishes.

Jas began returning the equipment to her bag, and in the space she cleared on the table, the woman placed the tray. Sayen felt like her stomach was going to climb up out of her throat to get something to eat.

"We aren't here to eat," Jas said. Sayen's stomach squirmed in disappointment. "Tell me how much you'll give us for our stuff."

"You don't trust me? You think I poisoned the food?" asked Erielle. "I'm hurt. Truly." She picked up a handful of rice and beans and pushed it in her mouth.

Sayen thought she heard Makey whimper with hunger.

"I bet the kid could eat something," Erielle said, her mouth full. "Couldn't you, hun?" She swallowed and took a bite from a piece of bread.

Makey's eyes reminded Sayen of her catdog—a genetically designed begging machine.

Jas sighed. "Oh, okay. Eat, everyone."

No one needed telling twice. Sayen leaned over to the table and helped herself. She'd eaten the rarest foods prepared by the world's top chefs in the fanciest restaurants, but nothing compared to the pleasure of eating at the underworlder's hangout that afternoon after two days of nothing but water.

While she and the others ate, Jas and Erielle negotiated the sale of the military items. Jas sneaked the odd piece of bread dipped in stew, and one or two leaf-wrapped parcels of spiced rice as they talked. The discussion took some time. Erielle had guessed that they were new to the underworld. As her talk with Jas spread to wider things, she filled them in on useful information about her society, such as the major forms of currency underworlders used to trade with when they had no creds to buy goods in shops.

A mild narcotic called kratom was most often used where a straight barter of goods wouldn't work, Erielle told them. She explained that the amount of food they were eating cost about twenty-five grams of kratom. An hour with someone whose main asset was their body cost about the same. Erielle paid her guards fifty grams of kratom a day, she said, but their bed and board were free.

Clothes and consumer products were mostly stolen, she told them without a shred of shame. Some underworld societies existed out of town, where a few crops were grown—mostly kratom. Electricity was 'diverted' from the main supply. Sayen strongly suspected that Erielle had a hand in many of the activities that kept her society running.

If you were an underworlder, Erielle explained, living there was mostly safe, though life was tough and children grew up fast. If you weren't an underworlder and you wandered into the territory, you were fair game. Most of the 'digifreaks', as Erielle called non-underworlders, came there to buy drugs or sex, but they took their chances on being robbed or worse.

When Sayen had taken the edge off her hunger, she began to wonder why Erielle was taking the time to explain all this to them. Why didn't she get what she wanted and show them the door?

"Thanks for telling us this," she said.

The woman's eyes flashed at her. One of them was slightly pulled out of shape by her scar. She ignored Sayen's interruption and returned to her conversation. Jas seemed to be getting tired of it, however, or maybe she was suspicious of Erielle's motives.

"Yeah, thanks for the information," she said, "and the food. But we really need to get going. So, what's your offer?"

"What's the hurry?" Erielle asked.

A muscle in Jas's jaw twitched.

"I'm going to buy everything you have," the underworlder continued, "and for a good price, but I want you to indulge me just a little longer." She got up and went to the door before bellowing down the stairs, "Sark, plates."

They waited in silence for the woman to come and clear the dishes. Makey had collapsed onto the cushions and was fast asleep. Guarded looks were passing between Jas and Carl, and Jas turned her gaze to Sayen, too, more than once. Her eyes warned her to be on guard.

When Sark had retreated, Erielle leaned her elbows on the table. "A Martian, an Australian, an offworlder—I think —and the cream of our genetically engineered society. Sounds like the start of a joke. But it's no joke to you, is it? I wasn't lying when I said I'd buy your stuff, and you're lucky you ran into me. I'm no angel, but I'm the best of my kind you'll find around here."

She reached over and took Jas's hand. Jas watched warily, but allowed the underworlder to turn it palm upward on the table. Erielle traced a slightly raised, almost imperceptible square bump on Jas's wrist with her finger. Jas's embedded credchip. "Do you know what people around here do for these?" Erielle asked. She reached higher and with the same finger she drew a line across Jas's throat. "You wouldn't have lasted the night if you hadn't happened to stumble in here. Weapons or not. Us under-worlders are very good at what we do, and we'd be prepared to risk a lot to get access to all your bank accounts, especially little ol' perfection over there. I bet you've got millions just sitting in an instant-access, haven't you, hun?"

Sayen shivered as the woman's eyes rested on her again.

"And don't imagine we'd do anything so refined as to force you to deposit everything you had in a reader. Oh no. We don't need your number to get past bank security. All we want is your chip, and certain people will get it whichever way is fastest. Lift your skin with a razor, cut off your hand, whatever. They'd kill you before or after. Doesn't matter to them, as long as you're not alive to tell anyone what happened."

Sayen was thankful that Makey wasn't listening to this. Even Jas looked taken aback.

"It's a bit of a shock to find out these things happen, isn't it? You don't hear about it on the vidnews. Stick around here a while, and you'll find out there's a lot of things you don't hear about on the vidnews."

The underworlder paused to take a small container out of her pocket. She opened it and took out a pill, which she swallowed without water. Jas frowned and drew back her hand. She glanced at Sayen and Carl.

"Where's the kid from?" Erielle asked.

"Dawn," Carl replied. "We picked him up from there when the planet was being attacked by Shadows."

Sayen wondered at the advisability of telling the underworlder about the Shadows. Though it was unlikely she'd had any dealings with them, there was nothing to be gained by being careless. But Erielle didn't pick up on the reference.

"Dawn?" she echoed, looking shocked. "I guessed he was from a colony, but I had no idea..." A flicker of sorrow crossed her face before she went on. "You said the planet was being attacked? What happened to the rest of the colonists?"

"Still there, the last we heard," Carl answered. "But the Government sent troops to defend them."

"What's Dawn got to do with you?" Jas asked.

The underworlder shook her head. "Just an old friend of mine went there." She smiled wryly. "I guess you think we're pretty strange living like this, don't you? Out of the system, no modding, no creds, no interfaces to glue our noses to day in, day out."

"I thought you didn't have a choice," said Jas.

"Everyone has a choice. Life's full of them. That's what you digifreaks don't realize. Sure, before you're born, your lives are laid out for you. Your parents program you with whatever looks, talents, intelligence they want, if they can afford it. You grow up indoctrinated into the system, scrambling for creds, watching the vids, believing the propaganda that passes for news. But even then, you have a choice—only you don't realize it. I had all that, but I turned my back on it. I chose this."

Tiredness was closing Sayen's eyelids. She yawned and

wondered why anyone would choose to live as the under-worlders did. Through half-open eyes, she glimpsed Jas throwing her a sharp glance.

"Still, it's easy to get taken in, I admit," continued Erielle. "A lot of people I used to know believed the Government's lies about Dawn being somewhere they could live freely and naturally. I lost a very special buddy because of that. Someone I loved. I didn't go with her. I didn't see why we couldn't or shouldn't live outside the system right here. It's a free planet, right?" She laughed.

Carl was also yawning.

"Sayen," Jas said, "wake up Makey. We're leaving."

"Hey, what's your problem?" asked Erielle. "We haven't decided a price yet."

Jas grabbed her bag and tried to stand, but stumbled. "You misborn," she muttered as she sank to her knees.

Carl toppled over, and Jas also hit the floor. Out of her control, Sayen's head fell forward. The last thing she heard before she lost consciousness was the underworlder's laughter.

7

———

It had been Sparks's idea, but he'd wanted Rogers to do the actual experiment. He thought he should find out if the Paths' flesh faded even when separated from the main body. But the truth was, his years at medical school had taught him that his strengths didn't lie in science. He was more comfortable in dealing with the face-to-face, human side of practicing medicine, not the nitty gritty of diagnosis, interpreting test results, and prescribing treatments. Emotions, he could do. Science, not so much.

After much persuasion, Rogers had agreed. He was in the Paths' quarantine chamber, wearing a biohazard suit. His air supply was provided by a long tube that stretched from the back of his suit to a unit on the wall. Not that any protection would save him from the onslaught of emotions the Paths would project when he approached them.

Sparks hadn't yet discovered how the telepathy worked. That was no surprise. Though telepathy was rare among intelligent species in the galaxy, it did exist, but no one had found out the substance or mechanism that transmitted brain waves from one mind to another. Not even the aliens who had telepathy had found the secret. It was one of the galaxy's great unsolved mysteries.

So Sparks hadn't expected to find out how the Paths transmitted. All he'd done was measure the effects. His results allowed him to predict just how Rogers was feeling right then.

"A lot of fear," came the man's voice over the intercom. Sparks checked that the interface was recording. "Getting stronger," Rogers said as he went closer to the Paths, holding aloft a scalpel. "Urgh, I don't know how you talked me into doing this, Sparks," he said. "I feel awful."

"Just a small sample, and you're done," Sparks replied into the mic. "I appreciate it, Rogers."

The man muttered to himself as he went closer. Sparks watched the Paths carefully. They were due to have one of their fading spells. Right on time, the creatures became slightly transparent. No change there. As usual, they didn't move, despite their obvious fear of the human getting closer to them, holding something metal and sharp.

Sparks felt a tiny bit sorry for the aliens. If he'd known how to administer an anesthetic, he would have. But it couldn't be helped. The sooner he found some useful information about the Paths to convey to Polestar, the better. He hoped that then he would be relieved of the assignment. It was well past time for the project to be handed over to real scientists.

"About to take a sample," said Rogers. His voice shook slightly. "I can tell you, it's certainly making me question my choice of profession, if this is how all my subjects feel."

"It'll be over in a moment," Sparks said in what he hoped was a reassuring tone.

The scalpel sliced into the flesh of a Path, and at the same moment, Rogers yelled. His arm began to shake as if he were fighting for control of it. He grunted as he lifted his hand and forced it down again to take a section of flesh.

His arms wobbling dangerously, Rogers transferred the tiny section to a glass microscope slide in his left hand. He tried to turn, but his legs also began to wobble. In a moment, he'd lost control of them, and he fell, dropping the slide and scalpel as he went down.

Sparks thumped an alarm on his interface and raced to the man's aid. He grabbed a hazard suit from the wall, hastily donned it, and sealed the flaps. He pulled open the door to the Paths' chamber and ran over to the prone Rogers. The man had fallen on the scalpel. It had pierced his suit and cut his thigh. Blood dripped from the wound, but it didn't look serious.

Rogers was in danger of contamination from exposure to the air of the room, which could contain anything the Paths might excrete as a defense mechanism. Sparks grabbed the man under his arms and began pulling him to the door. A couple of colleagues had turned up in response to the alarm. One of them lifted Rogers' legs, and they carried him out of the room between them.

Without waiting to remove Rogers' or their own hazard suits, they carried the affected man toward the station's medical center. Medics met them halfway with a gurney. They were also suited up.

Sparks and his colleague lifted Rogers onto the gurney, and one of the medics also leapt aboard and began cutting open the hazard suit. The other grabbed the bar and pushed the gurney, running with it down the corridor. Sparks also ran to keep up, watching as Rogers was cut free of his suit.

He couldn't understand what was wrong with him. The

cut from the scalpel hadn't looked too bad, and any emotional effects from contact with the Paths should have worn off by then. Yet Rogers was staring unblinking and apparently unseeing at the ceiling as he was rushed along. His mouth worked wordlessly, though Sparks could hear a faint droning hum or moan escaping his lips.

8

———

Jas reached up to her head as she woke. It hurt so much she was almost surprised to find it wasn't locked in a vise. She squinted against sunlight as she opened her eyes and registered that she was lying somewhere hard, cold, and bare. She tried to sit up. At the second attempt, she managed it and also closed her mouth, which had been open. Her gums and lips were painfully dry.

Krat. Krat. Krat. That misborn Erielle had drugged their food and taken the antidote herself before the drug had taken effect. She gasped as pain from her wrist registered. She looked down. It was covered in dried blood. Where her credchip had once been was now a raw gash. The impact of this discovery was beyond cursing to express. She could only stare at the wound for several moments as her heart and stomach plummeted to her feet.

She was sitting on a sidewalk, she realized. She turned to find her friends. All three were behind her in various states of consciousness. Makey was sitting up like her and staring in disbelief at his bloody wrist. Sayen was still out, and Carl was just opening his eyes.

Erielle and her crew had dumped them in an anonymous, empty street. Jas's bag was gone. Aside from the wounds in their wrists, the loss of their credchips didn't matter a lot. They couldn't use them without giving away their location, and it was only creds that they'd lost, not something more serious. But to have the chip physically removed was violating to a degree Jas had never experienced.

"What's happened?" Makey asked. "Did they cut that thing out of me?"

"Yeah, and me too," Jas replied. "All of us. The food was drugged."

"Krat," Carl mumbled.

Sayen awoke and gasped at the sight of her wrist.

"I only had mine put in a few days ago," Makey said. "Does that mean all our money's gone?"

"Bloody deros," said Carl as he sat up and checked out his wrist. "Yeah, they've got the lot."

"And everything we had to sell," Jas added.

"I guess we're lucky they didn't cut off our hands or kill us, like Erielle was saying," said Sayen.

"Guess so," said Jas, wondering why the woman hadn't done just that. She looked up at the sky between the roofs of the surrounding apartment blocks. "I reckon we've been out a couple of hours. Plenty of time for them to empty all our bank accounts. They won't have to worry about us reporting the crime now."

She couldn't believe what an idiot she'd been. Why had she gone into that woman's place? Why had she let the others eat the food and eaten it herself? How could she have been so stupid?

"What are we going to do now?" asked Makey.

Jas rubbed her face with her hands. The movement broke open her wrist injury, and a line of fresh blood snaked down her arm. She stood and pulled her shirt sleeve down over her wrist wound. "At least they left us our clothes."

"Erielle was right," said Sayen. "I do—or did—have millions of creds in my account. They could've given me some shoes at least."

This brought a subdued chuckle from the others. Carl held out his uninjured hand for Jas to help him to his feet. Jas gripped it tightly and pulled. Makey and Sayen also stood up.

"Well, my plans haven't come to much," said Jas. "What do you guys think we should do? I'm kratted if I know."

"We'll have to deal with the Shadows soon," Carl said. "We can't survive like this for long."

"Yeah, we haven't yet discussed just what we're going to do about them," said Sayen.

"It's hard to know *what* to do," said Jas. "Sayen, I never asked you what you found out about them when you were at the Security Headquarters."

"I told Carl while we were on the shuttle. The Government knows about them, but they've put a media ban on any mention of them. To avoid mass panic was the reason they gave, but I found a memorandum saying it was important to show the Transgalactic Council that they had the situation under control. The Council have been banning traffic to and from planets where the Shadows are known to be established. If I recall correctly, the Government didn't want to jeopardize Earth's trade agreements with other galactic nations."

"Misborns," Jas said.

"Oh, and those tests on Earth and Dawn that you two

took?" Sayen said to Jas and Carl. "Fake. Or mostly fake. There's only one test that actually works. It's a scanner, and it detects a glow around Shadows that no other species has. All the other tests are only to confuse the Shadows about what we're using to identify them."

"Really?" Carl said. "You didn't tell me that. I saw the same thing in the Shadow base. They were surrounded by a glow. Did you see it, Jas?"

"No. I didn't get a chance to notice much before one of them ran into me and got my goggles off as we struggled. What did you see?"

"It was just like Sayen says. A kind of aura. I wondered if it was an effect of the invisibility spray."

"Well, that might be useful information," said Sayen. "We can detect them if we have the right scanner. Then they can't hide by disguising themselves as our friends and relations."

"I wish I'd hidden that invisibility spray," said Jas, "instead of trying to sell it. I wonder if it was because you were looking through the spray on your goggles, Carl, or if the stuff altered your brain chemistry."

"No point in speculating right now," Sayen said. "What are we going to do about the Shadows? We can't find and destroy them all by ourselves, and I don't know who to tell about them. Who can we trust? It was a Shadow at the Global Government Security HQ who had me abducted, and I swear the Security Minister is a Shadow too. She was really creepy."

"If Earth's government is compromised," Jas said, "it seems to me we need to go one step higher."

"That's the Transgalactic Council, right?" Makey asked.

"Yeah," said Carl, "but how the hell we contact them, I don't know."

A hand clutched Jas's arm. It was Sayen. Her eyes were wide and her mouth was open. Jas followed her gaze and looked down the street. A group of underworlders had appeared at the end of it, and they were heading in their direction. Had Erielle decided that leaving them alive had been a mistake? Had she sent her cronies to finish them off?

"Shouldn't we run?" asked Makey.

"Not unless you want to be shot," Carl replied.

The underworlders were aiming weapons at them. They wouldn't stand a chance if they tried to escape, and they had nothing to defend themselves with. The only good news was that if Erielle had wanted them dead right away, the underworlders would have fired at them by then.

"You're coming with us," said one of them as soon as he was within speaking distance. They had no choice but to do as he said.

9

Erielle was a lot less friendly than she'd been earlier, in Makey's opinion. Instead of inviting them up to her room with the comfortable cushions, she had them shown into a basement. He didn't like the place. It was cold and damp and had no windows. His three friends also looked worried about what had happened, which didn't make him feel any better.

There wasn't even anywhere to sit down. All four of them stood waiting in silence, but they didn't have to wait long before the underworld leader appeared.

Her shaved head and narrow eyes were even more intimidating the second time round. Makey wondered why she'd called them back after drugging them and stealing those things called credchips. The amount given to him as his refugees' allowance had been so pitifully small, he wished she'd just asked him for it. It would have been a lot less painful than having the thing cut out of his wrist.

Erielle was standing with her arms folded across her chest. She pointed at him. "You," she said, "here." She lowered her hand to point at the ground next to her.

"No," cried the other three.

"You wanna argue about it?" asked Erielle. "I've got ten people with guns out there." She jerked a thumb toward the door. "You gonna fight me for him?"

"It's okay," Makey said. "I'll go."

He crossed the space and felt the pull of his friends' gaze as they looked at him across the divide. Erielle folded her arms again. "The people who I sent to download your creds have disappeared. I want to know where they've gone, and what you're going to do to help me get them back."

"We don't know where your friends are," said Jas, "but we can make a good guess at who's taken them."

"Who would that be?" asked Erielle. "And let me make it clear: if I find out you're lying, the kid here gets it."

"Geez, woman," Carl said, "why would we lie to you? The things that took your people would've taken us if we'd tried to use those chips."

"Things? What things?" Erielle asked.

"Shadows," Jas said, and she proceeded to tell the under-worlder what had happened aboard the starship *Galathea* and on Dawn. Carl and Sayen offered more information as she spoke. When they told Erielle about the Shadows on Dawn, Makey noticed her glance at him.

After half an hour or longer of explaining, Jas finished with their intention to try to contact the Transgalactic Council in the hope that they could help.

Jas stopped speaking, and Erielle seemed at a loss for words for a while. "Is this true, kid?" she asked Makey. When he nodded, she said, "But you would agree with them, wouldn't you?" She deliberated a little while longer before sighing and saying, "It's so bizarre, I don't think anyone could make it up. I guess I believe you."

"So will you help us?" asked Jas.

"What do you mean?"

"We have to do something to stop the Shadows. You can help us get a message to the Transgalactic Council. We can't do it by ourselves. You saw what happened as soon as someone tried to use the credchips that identified them as us. We can't go to the Government because we don't know who we can trust."

Erielle snorted with laughter. "Me? Help you digifreaks? Your kind have been making our lives a misery for centuries. All we ever wanted to do was live the way we wanted—naturally. And what did you do? You ruined our Earth for us. You made us the lowest of the low. We have no respect, no voice, and no power. Naturals are shunned and ridiculed wherever they go.

"*Help* you? Forget it. You can all go to hell. These Shadows you're so worried about won't be interested in us underworlders. According to what you say, they prey on people in authority or who have something they want. We don't have anything to offer them. Who knows? Maybe they'll turn out to be better masters than our current ones." She winked sardonically. "No, I think you've told me enough. I'll do what I can to get my people back from these Shadows, though it sounds like there isn't much hope. I should have known to steer clear of digifreaks. They only ever bring trouble."

She turned to Makey. "You can stay with me. I made a mistake in letting you go with them. You belong here with us. You understand our beliefs, and as a son of a Dawner, I owe it to your parents to look after you."

"I don't want to stay here," Makey said. "I want to go with my friends."

"That's a bad idea," said Erielle. "If you go with them,

you'll die. No one survives outside digifreak society without help."

"I don't care. They're still my friends, and they saved my life more than once. I trust them. I don't trust you. Look what you did to me," he exclaimed, lifting his arm and pulling down his sleeve. The wound was thick with dried blood.

Erielle looked down. "I'm sorry. I wasn't thinking. I was forgetting that you were one of us."

"I'm not one of you," exclaimed Makey. "This isn't what the people of Dawn were about. I don't know what you underworlders think, but this life doesn't have anything to do with living naturally and caring for Earth Mother. I don't believe in that stuff, but even I know that."

"He's got a point," said Carl.

Erielle scowled at him. She turned to Makey. "After you've lived with us for a while, you'll understand."

"How many times do I have to tell you? I'm *not* living with you. And I'm not going to be lied to anymore. I've had enough of that. What are you going to do to make me stay? Are you planning on keeping me a prisoner here? Is *that* what being an underworlder's about? Keeping kids locked up?"

Erielle bit her lip. "No, I won't keep you prisoner. You're right. That isn't the underworlder way, unless—"

"Unless you aren't underworlders, like my friends. It's one rule for you and another for everyone else," Makey interjected contemptuously. He was amazed to see the older woman redden slightly. He hadn't been trying to embarrass her. He was only angry at the idea of being separated from his friends, and he'd said what he really thought.

"You're wrong if you think the Shadows won't come after you," Jas said. "When we first encountered them, they went after the highest in command, it's true. But we had every reason to believe they would have gone for the entire crew eventually, and then they would have returned to Earth aboard our ship to help infest the planet. I can't think why they wouldn't work their way through the whole of Earth's population eventually and replace even underworlders with their kind. Look at what happened to the people who tried to use our credchips. It's already started.

"Erielle, I get what you're saying about what your people suffer. I really do, and these last few hours have opened my eyes to things I was never aware of, but believe me when I say this isn't an 'us and them' thing. We have to put away our differences and work together if we're going to defeat these aliens. It's going to take everything we've got."

Holding up a hand to Jas, Erielle said, "Okay, okay, enough. I need to think. You can all stay here tonight. I'll get some food sent in." Reacting to the looks on their faces, she added, "Drug-free food. You have my word."

She left them. Carl went over to Makey and ruffled his hair. "Nice one, kid."

Makey grinned. Finally, he'd done something useful.

10

———

Sparks stood nervously outside Rogers' room. The nurse had told him that the lab tech had shown signs of coming around, and he peered at the man lying in the isolation room. He was worried about what Polestar would make of the incident. He might be held responsible.

Inside his room, Rogers smacked his lips lazily, and his eyes half opened. Sparks felt a surge of relief. He pressed the intercom button. "Rogers, can you hear me? Are you awake?"

"Hmmm...who's that?"

"It's me, Sparks. How are you feeling?"

Rogers tried to rise, but slumped back down onto his bed. "Where am I? What's happened? Oh, wait, I remember. The Paths."

"Yes, that's right. You're still on the station, in the medical center. How are you feeling? You had some kind of fit."

"I did, did I?" Rogers, with some effort, managed to rise to his elbows. He scanned the room until he spotted the observation window Sparks was looking through. "There you are. How long have I been out?"

"Four and a quarter hours. Do you remember what happened? You'd just taken a sample when you passed out."

"Hmmm...yes, I do remember." The lab tech reclined on his pillows. "I was in a state of terrible fear, brought on by the Paths. Urgh...it was awful feeling their terror. I think they thought I was going to kill them. I'm never doing that again. So don't even think of asking me." His eyes swiveled to the right to meet Sparks's.

"No, of course I won't," Sparks said.

"Good. So...I cut once, and then again to take the sample, and I thought that was it. Their ordeal would be over, and I would be able to get out of range of those odd creatures, and then...then, well...I was suddenly in the most wonderful place I've ever been."

"Really?" asked Sparks. "What do you mean? You didn't go anywhere—except straight here to the medical center as fast as we could take you. You must have been hallucinating."

"I suppose I must have, but that isn't how it felt. It felt very real. I was floating in infinite space. And...now, let me see...I seem to remember that I was sure *I* could become infinite too, and fill the space. Or I could choose to become infnitesimally small. But that wasn't the best part, oh no. I was serenely, blissfully happy. The happiest I've ever been in my entire life. No cares or worries bothered me. Nothing mattered at all, except *being*, you know?" His face seemed to shine as he relived the memory. "Ahhh...it was quite wonderful. I wouldn't mind going there again, in fact, if it were possible."

"Extraordinary," Sparks mused. The Paths had accessed the technician's emotions, but not as he would have expected when they were under threat. He would have expected them to continue to project their negative emotions in order to make whatever was threatening them go away. They'd projected their fear of the approaching lab tech with his scalpel, as he'd expected, but when the lab tech actually assaulted them, they'd overwhelmed him with bliss.

Their strategy had been effective. The result was that Rogers collapsed and didn't cut them again. But as a long-term behavior, it didn't make much sense. The creatures were providing a reward in response to attacks. Wouldn't a hostile species that experienced the reward be tempted to attack again?

"Sparks," Rogers said. "Are you listening? I said, do you know how long they plan to keep me here?"

"Sorry, I was miles away. I don't know how long you'll be here, I'm afraid. Until they're sure you haven't been infected by an agent from the Paths, maybe? When you collapsed, your scalpel cut through your hazard suit. You've been exposed."

"Bugger," Rogers said. "Oh well. I suppose it means I get out of work for a while."

"Yes, enjoy it while you can," said Sparks. "I'll let the nurse know you're awake. I'll be back later to check how you're doing. Is there anything you need?"

"I don't think so. I'll call the nurse if I do."

"Okay. Rogers, one more thing before I go. I'm curious about this state you were in. Do you think you could write me a report about it?"

"Doesn't look like I'm going to have much else to do for a while."

"Great. Thanks."

"You know," Rogers said, "I was a little peeved at having

to go near the Paths again. Those creatures give me the willies. I like my emotions to stay my own. But now, I'm kind of glad you asked me to help out. Whatever it was they did to me, I'm glad I had the experience. I doubt I'll ever forget it."

It was the quiet shift, and after Sparks left Rogers, his words helped Sparks sleep more easily. The man was positive about his experience, and Sparks hoped he wouldn't have too much explaining to do. He also had something especially interesting to put in his next report to Polestar. With a little luck, the company would hand the project on to the big league xenobiologists now that he'd discovered something unusual.

The following morning, on his way to the canteen to eat breakfast, he passed the Paths' quarantine chamber and found the whole place, including his observation office, had been sealed off with security tape. The master of the quarantine station was there, and when he spotted Sparks he approached him and slapped him on the shoulder. "Just the man I wanted to see. I comm'd you three times. Is your button turned off?"

Sparks looked down at the comm button on his shirt. He had indeed accidentally thumbed it off as he was attaching the device. He turned it on. "Yes, sorry. What's going on? Why's the area been cordoned off? Has something happened to the Paths?" He wondered if Rogers had harmed them somehow when he'd taken his sample. Maybe they'd bled out over night. He hadn't gone back to check on them because he'd been too preoccupied with the lab tech.

"I thought you hadn't heard. One of the researchers broke into the Path chamber during the quiet shift."

"What?" exclaimed Sparks. "Why would anyone do that?"

"As far as we can tell, it was because she'd heard about Rogers' experience yesterday. He told the nurse, and she passed the story on. She didn't see any reason not to, she says, and I guess she's right. It was just a little bit of gossip to her. The poor woman; she's distraught now. She's saying it was all her fault."

"What was her fault?" asked Sparks, standing on his tiptoes and craning to look into the chamber.

"The researcher got it into her head that what happened to Rogers sounded pretty nice, and she thought she'd like to try it herself."

Sparks's eyes grew round. "No."

"Yes. She took a knife with her. I don't know what she intended. Thankfully, she didn't have the opportunity to do much damage."

"I'm glad to hear it," said Sparks. "I take it they weren't too badly cut?"

"They were hardly cut at all."

"And the woman? Did she have a fit like Rogers? I take it you've placed her in confinement?" He leaned closer and lowered his voice. "Is she a natural by any chance? I've always thought there should be some kind of vetting for professional positions."

"No. The reason she didn't cut the Paths very much was because she didn't have the opportunity. She died."

"She's dead? They killed her?" Sparks almost squeaked.

"She's lying in there right now. She was cold by the time someone noticed the chamber door was open. She'd used her security clearance to disable the alarm."

"Dead?" Sparks repeated. He needed to sit down.

He pushed past the master and stepped over the tape that covered the door to his observation room. Collapsing into his chair, he caught sight of the deceased administrator in the Paths' quarantine chamber. She was right next to them. They hadn't moved or changed position, but the woman was on her back, her arms and legs spread out. The most beautiful smile Sparks had ever seen was emblazoned across her features.

11

———

"What are you planning to tell the Transgalactic Council, if you ever manage to contact them?" Erielle asked. The day following their capture, Sayen and the others had been allowed to climb the stairs to her private room once more. Though, from the way Erielle continued to ignore her, Sayen doubted she would have received the same respect if she'd been alone.

"We'll tell them what's been happening here on Earth," Jas said. "We'll tell them the Shadows have infiltrated the Global Government, and that whoever hasn't been killed and replaced believes that the problem was dealt with, and the Shadows are no longer a threat."

"That's a long message." Erielle smiled sardonically. "And why would the Council believe you?"

Jas had been resting her elbows on the low table that separated the two women. She leaned back. "Why would they believe us? Why wouldn't they? It isn't the sort of thing someone would make up."

"You don't think so? There's plenty of crazies around.

Sometimes modding goes wrong, you know. Some people aren't right in the head, and they often end up here. Plenty of conspiracy theorists. The Council wouldn't take much persuading from someone high up in government to convince them that you're insane. Hell, I bet they receive a thousand messages a day from crackpots in one corner of the galaxy or another. Why do you think they'd treat yours any differently?"

Jas frowned and looked down.

"What do *you* think we should do?" Carl asked.

"I'm not sure. Tell me more about these aliens."

They told her all they knew, and when they arrived at Sayen's investigations at the Global Government Security HQ, she took over the story and related what she'd read in the hidden files. She also explained how her manager, Bernie, had turned out to be a Shadow and had arranged for her to be abducted and nearly replaced by a Shadow herself. Erielle didn't look at her as she spoke, but she listened.

"So you can identify Shadows, no matter how closely they resemble their victim, with one of these special scanners?" she asked.

"That's what I read," Sayen replied.

"And that's what I saw, too, when we rescued Sayen," said Carl. "We were covered in that invisibility spray you stole from us."

"Ha, consider it payment for your bed and board," Erielle replied. "Well, we can't use that. That's long gone down the pipeline. Much too hot to keep. But if you had a scanner, you could identify a Shadow and capture it. A Shadow found in Earth territory would be good evidence to show the Council."

"We don't need to identify a Shadow," Sayen said. "I know one. The man I was working under at the Security HQ. If he's still there, we could try to kidnap him."

"That British guy you were telling us about?" Carl asked.

"Well, that's who the victim was, yes," Sayen replied. "Now, a Shadow's doing a great impersonation of him. Unless that thing's gone somewhere else, he'll be at the HQ."

"Yeah," said Jas, "we could kidnap a Shadow to prove we aren't crazy. But what then? How would we get it to the Transgalactic Council?"

"One thing at a time," Erielle said.

"It's some kind of a plan," Carl said. "Sayen, the HQ's in this city, right? How far from here?"

"Not far. About half an hour by autocab."

"I can't think of a better alternative," Jas said. "Let's do it. Tonight. The longer we wait, the more people will fall victim, and the Shadows will move closer to catching us. Sayen, think of everything you can remember about this creature. What time it leaves the office. How it goes home— if that's where it goes. We'll ambush it in a quiet spot if we can. Erielle, how many of your people can you lend us?"

"People? You can't have any of my people. You're on your own."

"What?" Makey exclaimed. "I thought you were going to help us."

"I *am* helping you. By letting you and your friends go. That's what you wanted, wasn't it? I've had your wrists treated. I've even listened to your cockeyed plans and pointed out how stupid they are. What more do you want from me?"

"I expected you to help us defeat the Shadows," said Makey. "Don't you want them forced to leave Earth? My friends told you what happened on Dawn. You said there was someone you loved there. Don't you care about what happened to them?"

Erielle's brief expression of sadness was quickly followed by a stony look. "My lover made her choice. She could have stayed here and continued to fight the Government, but she didn't. She left with the rest of the Earth Mother cultists. I learned my lesson then. Look after yourself. No one else matters. The Transgalactic Council doesn't give a krat about us underworlders. If these Shadows come to us, we'll fight them. But we'll fight on our terms and in our own way, not because some digifreaks want us to."

Jas sighed and shook her head. "Will you give us our weapons back at least? Explosives? You know we'll need everything we can get."

Erielle said, "Okay." She looked at Makey. "Are you sure you won't stay here with me? I was hoping we could talk about Dawn. Maybe you knew my friend. I'd have liked to hear news of her."

"I haven't changed my mind. I know who my friends are, and I know the right thing to do, even if you don't."

The corner of Erielle's lip lifted. "You sound just like my friend. Maybe you did know her."

"I think you should stay here, Makey," Jas said. "In fact, I insist. I'm not allowing you to come along."

"What?"

"Like I told you in Antarctica when you ignored my order, you're a danger to yourself and others. I can't trust you, so you aren't coming with us."

"Oh, come on, Jas," said Carl.

"And like I told *you*, this is none of your business."

Carl let out a snort of frustration and folded his arms.

Sayen said tentatively, "Jas—"

"No. This isn't up for discussion. The kid isn't coming with us. He's too young, and he's too unreliable. I'm not going to risk both your lives or mine so he can feel good about himself."

"It isn't about feeling good about myself," Makey exclaimed, rising to his feet and clenching his fists. "Those misborns killed my mam and my sister. I want to fight them just as much as you do."

"Hey," shouted Erielle, "simmer down." When their gazes turned to her, she continued, "I changed my mind. The kid goes with you, or you don't get any of your stuff back. I'm not having digifreaks telling us underworlders what we can and can't do. The kid goes with you, or you leave here now with nothing but the clothes on your backs."

Jas glared at the woman.

"Take it or leave it," Erielle said.

Carl said, "We'll take it, right, Sayen?"

"Yes, we'll take Makey with us," she replied. "Give us our things, and we'll get along." Time was passing. The Shadow Bernie would be leaving work soon, and they didn't yet have a plan for his capture. Sayen also felt Jas was being unreasonable. Most of the time, she was nice, but sometimes she could be pig-headed. She didn't know what her problem was.

Erielle called for the weapons and explosives she'd taken from them and handed them over to Jas. The woman took them without a word. She looked furious.

Sayen had another problem that needed addressing urgently. "Erielle, do you think I could get some shoes?" she asked, pointing at her bare, dirty feet. The sight of them made her squirm. What wouldn't she give for a hot bath and clean clothes as well?

Rolling her eyes, Erielle made the request by her usual

method of shouting downstairs. Almost miraculously, a worn pair of running shoes arrived that were only about a size too big. Sayen slipped them on and tied the laces, trying hard not to think about the residue from someone else's feet that was touching her skin.

12

Erielle not only returned everything she'd taken from them besides the invisibility spray, but she also loaned them one of the strange self-driving cars the underworlders used and gave them a map to a safe, unoccupied house on the edge of her territory. She said they could use it as long as they wanted.

Carl was pleased at the loan of the car. He loved driving cars. He'd learned how when he was in his early teens, when self-drivers had already been mostly replaced by auto-drive cars. A couple of old relics lived among the farm machinery in the barn. Charging their batteries took forever because they were so old, but it was worth the wait to be in control of a vehicle instead of being carried around like a baby.

Jas and Carl sat in front. Sayen and Makey were in the back with the bag of equipment between them. The light was beginning to fail.

"You sure you can handle this?" asked Erielle, leaning down to look through the car window.

"Yeah, no problem," Carl said as he searched for the

headlight switch. He tried one, and the windscreen wipers started up. He tried another, and the windows closed. Erielle stepped back to avoid being decapitated. The third switch he tried turned on the headlights, though their beams were weak.

Carl lowered the windows. "Got it. Are you sure we won't be stopped by the police? Are these cars still legal?"

"They're still legal, but, yeah, you might be stopped. I don't know what you can do about that. I guess you'll just have to take the chance. You could always walk there, but it'd take hours, and I don't know how you'll kidnap a Shadow without a vehicle. You can't hire an autocab without ID. This is the best y'all can do, I reckon."

"I think you're right," Carl said. "We'll get going."

"Good luck," Erielle said. "Take care, kid," she said to Makey. "Remember, there's always a place for you here. I'd like to hear about Dawn sometime."

"I'll come back and tell you all about it."

"You look after him," Erielle said to the others.

"Thanks for the shoes," Sayen said.

Erielle didn't reply. She stepped back. Jas also said nothing. She sat with her arms folded, staring ahead.

Carl didn't know what was the matter with her, and he wasn't sure that he even cared. She had a mood on, and like always, she wouldn't open up about whatever was bothering her. He'd thought they might have had something going after they'd nearly kissed back at the farm in Australia, but ever since they'd rescued Sayen, the coldness of Antarctica seemed to have crept into her bones and heart.

"Got your seat belts on?" he asked the group generally as he searched for the button to start the engine.

"All buckled up," came Sayen's response from behind him.

"Hey, Sayen," Carl said, "you know where we're going, right? Why don't you come sit up front here and direct me?"

"Sure," Sayen replied, and she and Jas swapped seats.

Jas's knees pushed into Carl's back as she squeezed into the smaller space. He preferred that slight discomfort to her taciturn presence beside him. He started the engine, and the former navigator gave her first set of directions.

As they gradually drove farther and farther from the underworlders' domain, the traffic became heavier and pedestrians grew sparse. It wasn't long before they were driving through the business district, attracting many second glances in their out-of-date, self-drive vehicle. Carl grew nervous. Surely it wouldn't be long before they were stopped. As soon as they were asked for their IDs, the game would be over.

"Second left," Sayen said. "We're a few minutes' walk from the Security HQ, but I don't recall any parking nearby. Not public parking anyway. And we would never pass the security check to get into the underground car park. But if I'm right, there's an alley down this street," she said as Carl turned the vehicle. "We can wait there until it's time for Shadow Bernie to leave work."

Dusk was falling, and the street lights were turning on.

On their way over, Sayen had explained that their target usually left the office around seven o'clock every evening and departed in his personal government car. Because Sayen left by heli, she'd never seen the car, so she wasn't totally sure that what he'd told her was true.

"It's over there," she said to Carl, pointing to a narrow, dark opening on the left-hand side of the street.

He indicated and pulled in. The alley was only as wide as the car. Tall office blocks rose on either side. There was no exit except for the busy street at the other end of the alley. Carl didn't drive far in. With nowhere to turn around, he would have to reverse the car out.

"What's the time?" asked Jas, leaning between the front seats.

The car clock read six thirty.

"We don't have long," she continued. "The Shadow might leave work early, and we can't risk a practice run. It won't be long before someone reports us for suspicious behavior. We have to get the Shadow tonight. Do you have any idea what direction it might go?" she asked Sayen.

"I don't."

"Then we'll have to watch the car park exit and follow its car when it leaves," said Jas.

"It's not going to be easy," Carl said. He looked at the falling darkness in the alley. "What if the car windows are tinted?"

"We just have to do our best," said Sayen. "We don't have to wait very near the exit. My eyes can zoom in, though I can't see through darkened windows."

"Okay," Jas said. "When we spot the Shadow, we follow it until we're in a quieter part of the city. Then I'll shoot out the car wheels. As soon as the car stops, we've got to move fast. We won't have long until the police get there. But be careful. We don't know what weapons it might be carrying, and there might be more than one of them in the car."

"Right," Carl said. "Sounds like we're all set. Sayen, where do we go from here?"

After she gave him the final directions, he reversed out of the alley. They had to wait a while for a pause in the traffic before he could enter the street and pull away. Following Sayen's instructions, he drove them to a spot about fifty meters from the Security HQ car park exit. It was at the back of the building, and the street only served the car park so there was no other traffic. They waited.

The exit was automated. No visible human guard threatened to become curious about their presence, but Carl was sure that cameras would be covering the street. It was the Global Government Security Headquarters, after all. They wouldn't have long before they were challenged. He hoped their target wasn't working overtime that night.

A light flashed, signaling that a car was about to leave. A limousine appeared, its windows tinted black. There was an audible sigh of frustration from everyone. Would they ever be able to recognize the Shadow? Automation had done away with the need for transparent windows in cars. What if the entire Government fleet was the same?

The limousine left at the opposite end of the street from them. The light at the exit flashed again, and another car appeared. It was an unmarked van. Carl's stomach tightened as the van turned in their direction. Was this a security van coming to check them out? The van passed, though two women sitting in the front seats gave them curious looks. Once it had passed them, Carl's stomach relaxed.

A third car appeared. This car's windows were transparent, and Carl could make out one person sitting in the front seat.

"Is that him?" Jas asked Sayen.

"No, it's just another of the Government personnel."

The car turned toward them. As it drew closer and the occupant's face became more distinct to Carl, his heart skipped a beat. He knew this person. Where did he know him from? As the answer came, he felt the blood drain from his face.

"That's not your Shadow??" he asked Sayen.

"No, I'm sure. Shadow Bernie's much older. But I recognize him. I saw him on my first day."

"Look away," Carl barked as the car drew closer. He turned to face the back of the car, looking into Jas's puzzled eyes. She bent her head down as the car passed.

Carl's heartbeat quickened as he watched the car driving away in the reflection of his rear view mirror. He noted which way it turned as it left the street. He put the car into drive, turned the steering wheel, and followed.

"What are you doing?" cried Jas. "Sayen said that's not him."

"It might not be Sayen's Shadow, but it's a Shadow all right," Carl said. "It's Alef from the *Galathea*."

13

———

"**W**ho the krat's Alef?" Jas asked as Carl sped down the street. The acceleration pushed her back into her seat.

"Alef from geo-phys," Carl replied.

"I knew I'd seen him before," exclaimed Sayen, "but I couldn't remember from where. I didn't recognize him out of uniform, and I was only with him for a couple of minutes."

"Geo-phys like Margret?" Jas asked. "I was right. There was another Shadow aboard the ship. So he went into the trap with her and got replaced at the same time?"

"Yep, he must have," answered Carl. "You remember when we were trying to get onto the bridge? It was Alef who helped me tackle Loba, before the misborn got away from me. I left Alef behind when I chased after him."

"But why would he help you take down Loba if he was a Shadow himself?" asked Jas.

"I dunno. Maybe he had a problem with him, or he saw that things were going south and decided to play the long game. Whatever his plan was, it worked. He made it all the way here with us, and now he's joined his mates in the Global Government."

Carl pulled out into the rush hour traffic. His head was fixed firmly ahead as he kept his eyes on the Shadow's car. Jas stopped talking to him to let him concentrate on following their target. She opened the bag next to her and took out a weapon. Tapping Sayen on her shoulder, she passed the weapon forward to her. She took another for herself and peered around Carl's head. He was drawing closer to the Shadow's car, though four or five vehicles separated them.

"What about me?" asked Makey.

Jas frowned and took the third and final gun out of the bag. "Self-defense only," she said as she handed it to the kid.

They were leaving the inner city district, and the roads were becoming quieter. Jas wondered where the Shadow was going. Did the Shadows continue their pretense of being human and return to their victims' homes each night? Or did they have a secret meeting place where they all congregated?

Houses and apartment blocks of a residential district surrounded them. Carl had moved their car closer, and they were only two cars away from the Shadow's vehicle. Jas hoped the strangers' cars that lay between them and the Shadow's would leave that road soon. They'd been following it for a while; she worried that it might have noticed them.

"Can you get around these cars, Carl?" she asked.

"I can, but overtaking on a street like this would be too noticeable. It's better that I stay back a little while longer."

Jas rubbed the edge of her weapon nervously. She had those prickles she always got when something bad was going to happen. But she couldn't do anything about it.

They had to go ahead with the plan. They wouldn't get a second chance.

"Be careful, everyone," she said. "And Makey, let us handle this. Stay in the car."

The kid tutted.

"Here we go," Carl said as one of the intervening cars turned down a side road. At the next exit, the second car did the same. There was nothing between them and the car in front carrying the Shadow Alef.

Jas checked over her shoulder. A few vehicles were behind them, but it couldn't be helped. She hoped they would get out of danger fast when the shooting started. She and the others would only have a couple of minutes to snatch the Shadow before the police arrived.

"I think he's seen us," Carl said. "He keeps turning to look back."

"Right, let's go," Jas said. "Drive up his ass, Carl."

She lowered her window, and Sayen lowered hers. Jas undid her seatbelt so that she could lean out and take aim. She fired. Her shot went wide, but Sayen's hit true, taking out the back wheel of the Shadow's vehicle. The car began to veer across the road. Jas fired again and hit the front wheel on the same side as the car turned its longer side toward them. The Shadow ducked down and disappeared from view.

An explosion sounded from behind Jas, and their car rocked. "Krat," shouted Carl. The car began to swerve. "We're being shot at. We've got Shadows behind us."

Jas's stomach fell as she turned. The van that had passed them outside the Security HQ car park was right behind them. While they'd been following the Shadow Alef's car, they'd been followed themselves. She reversed her aim and shot at the window of the Shadow van. The beam melted a hole in the plastiglass and hit one of the Shadows in the chest. It fell to one side, but the van continued on.

Their own rear window was hit by a shot from the remaining Shadow's weapon, and the car filled with smoke and the acrid stench of burning plastic.

They crashed. Jas was thrown forward into the back of Carl's seat. As she sat up, she saw that they'd hit the Shadow Alef's vehicle, which straddled the road. Carl revved the engine and backed up so fast that Jas was thrown forward again. Her weapon was knocked from her grasp and fell onto the floor.

She bent down to pick it up. Sayen was firing and the tires of their car screeched as Carl did a u-turn and pulled away. Jas was rocked backward, but managed to grasp the fallen weapon. As she regained her seat, she noticed that the handle was sticky with something.

They were heading toward the Shadows' van. It was heading toward them. Carl sped up, seemingly intent on meeting the other vehicle head on. Jas leaned out of her window and fired at the Shadow in the front of the van. She didn't hit it, but it had to lean over to avoid her blast, and its own shot went wide.

The van filled her vision. They were going to hit it. But at the last split second, it pulled to one side. As they flew past, they clipped its wing. They sped into the night.

They'd escaped.

They'd failed to catch a Shadow, but at least they'd gotten away alive. The wind from their open windows blew away the smoke in the car. Wondering what the sticky stuff was, Jas turned her weapon around in her hand. In the dark street it looked black, but as they drove under a streetlight she saw that it was red. Blood. Her weapon was covered in blood.

Had she been hit? She quickly checked herself. She didn't think so. Her heart stopped as she realized Makey hadn't said anything for a while. Hardly daring to look, she turned her gaze to the kid. His eyes were closed and his head lolled to the side. His front was soaked in the blood running from his neck.

14

They screeched to a halt outside Erielle's place. Sayen leapt from the car and bolted down the alley that led to Erielle's door. She hammered on it and screamed. Carl was on her heels, carrying Makey in his arms. Jas had her hands pressed to Makey's neck, but the blood wouldn't stop steadily leaking out. His face was white. By the time Carl reached the door, it had been opened by one of Erielle's guards. The man's puzzled face changed to one of alarm when he saw the wounded kid.

"What is it?" Erielle asked, appearing at the bottom of the stairs. She gave a look of horror as she spotted Makey. "In here," she said, opening a door. Carl carried him over and Jas followed, her hands still clasped to the kid's neck.

Erielle spat, "I told you to take care of him."

"And I didn't want him to come," Jas retorted, shouldering Erielle aside as she went into the room.

It was a makeshift medical treatment room, containing a couple of outdated hospital beds, a glass cabinet of bottled drugs, drawers labeled with the names of medical equipment, and some basic medical devices and instruments.

Carl laid Makey down on one of the beds. Jas had the heel of one hand on his neck, and the other heel pressed on the first, but blood dripped onto the sheet.

"He got hit by a shot from Shadows behind us," Jas said. "He didn't say a thing. Maybe he passed out immediately. He's lost a lot of blood."

"I can see that," snapped Erielle. "He's in shock. He needs a transfusion."

"Can you do that here?" Sayen asked.

"We could if we had any blood, but we've had a few accidents to treat. We used the last of it just yesterday. Krat."

"We can give him ours," said Sayen.

"Do you know what blood type he is?" Erielle asked.

"No," Sayen replied. "I don't think he has any medical records either. He only arrived on Earth a few weeks ago."

"He needs universal donor blood," Jas said.

"I know," said Erielle. She bit her lip. "We usually steal it, but it's a complicated operation. He can't wait. We'll have to do a smash and grab. It won't be easy, but we have to try. I'll go now. Keep the pressure on his neck. If his heart stops, there's a defibrillator in that cupboard." She turned to leave.

"I'll come with you," Sayen said. "I can help."

"No. Stay here. You'll only get in the way."

"No, she won't," said Jas. "Take her. You can use her. Believe me."

Erielle looked doubtful, but she didn't offer any more objections. As she left, Sayen followed close behind.

They took the car Carl had driven. Two more underworlders came with them. Sayen sat in the back and fastened her belt. Erielle sat in the front with the driver. As the car pulled away, they closed the doors. They were soon speeding through the streets.

"There's a clinic a few minutes away," said Erielle. "They

have artificial universal donor blood. I know because we have someone on the inside who supplies us. But the clinic's closed for the evening. We'll have to break in."

"I might be able to disable the security," Sayen said.

"I'll give you a minute to try," Erielle replied. "If you can't do it..." She pulled out a weapon with a huge muzzle, "...we blast our way in."

The underworlder sitting next to Sayen said, "There's a police station right around the corner. We won't have time to get away before they catch us."

"We have to try, or that kid's gonna die," Erielle said.

The underworlder muttered to himself.

They arrived. The clinic was a small place, only serving the immediate neighborhood, it seemed to Sayen. It stood on the street corner. A high, metal-paneled fence ran down the side. The frontage was solid brick except for a glass door. As they passed, Sayen could see a receptionist's desk and a few chairs in the waiting room.

They pulled up a few doors down and walked back to the clinic's entrance. It was securely locked. Inside, the light of the alarm panel winked. There was no way to access the security control from the outside.

"Better blast it," said one of the underworlders.

"I bet that door's laser-proofed," Sayen said, "if they're storing drugs in a neighborhood like this."

The underworlder looked offended, but Erielle said, "She's probably right."

"What about around the back?" asked Sayen.

"The fence is four meters high. We'll never get over it," said the underworlder.

"Speak for yourself," said Sayen. "Give me the blaster," she said to Erielle. The woman hesitated before handing it over.

Sayen trotted around the side of the building. The underworlder's estimation of the height of the fence was about right. She crossed to the other side of the street and sized it up. When Erielle and the underworlders appeared, she called, "Bring the car around," and ran toward the fence.

A few steps before she reached it, she jumped, springing from her right foot. She sailed up and caught the top of the fence with her fingertips. Quickly pulling herself up, she climbed over before landing in the yard behind the medical center. The fence cast the place in deep shadow. Sayen blinked her eyes to night vision, and the scene swam into a green-hued view.

The yard was bare save for garbage bins bearing signs for different kinds of medical waste. The back door was locked tight, and like in the front, there were no windows.

She had no choice but to try to blast the door. Laser-proofing was expensive. Maybe they wouldn't have taken the extra precaution with the back door. It would trigger the alarm, but she couldn't help that. She pulled the blaster from the waistband of her pants and fired it, concentrating its beam on the door lock. The metal glowed red, then white. That had to have triggered the alarm. Sayen wondered how long she had before the police responded. Probably less than a minute.

She threw her shoulder against the door, bursting it open. Not slowing her pace, she sped through and into the center. As she went, she realized that she should have asked Erielle where they kept the blood. Too late for that. But the clinic was small. The blood shouldn't be too hard to find.

She was in some kind of consulting room. Various scanners and other medical equipment stood against all the walls. Where did they keep the medical supplies? She threw open another door. She was in the doctor's office, with a simple bed, the physician's desk and interface, and chairs. Sayen ran through, upending a chair as she tripped over it in her hurry.

Flinging open another door, she found herself in the waiting room she'd seen from the front. Bright lights oscillated over the walls, shining in from outside. The police had arrived. A car door slammed. They were coming over to the clinic. Did they have a key to the place?

Where were the supplies? Sayen spotted another door. She sped through it. At last, she was in the supply room. It was full of cabinets and refrigerator units. All were locked, but they bore signs. Her eyes roved feverishly. She must have only seconds. She saw it.

Sayen grasped the handle of the unit containing the blood bank and forced it down. The lock snapped off, and the door opened. She grabbed handfuls of bags of artificial blood, expecting every moment to feel a police officer's hand on her shoulder.

She raced out. Passing through the waiting room, she caught sight of an officer standing outside the front door, looking in. At the same moment, the officer saw her. He raised his hand to his belt and shouted. Sayen ran out of the waiting room door in a heartbeat, through the office and treatment room, and outside into the yard.

"Hey, catch these," she yelled and flung the bags of blood over the fence, praying that the others were still there and waiting; praying that they were good at catching.

From behind her came the sound of movement. The police were in the building. She had to jump the fence immediately, but the yard was small. She had hardly any room for a running start. She backed to the clinic, ran, and leapt. She didn't make it to the top of the fence. Her fingers tried to grasp the smooth panels before she slipped down and landed heavily.

"Stop where you are. You're under arrest," shouted a police officer.

She had less than a couple of seconds before it was all over. Sayen took another run at the fence. This time, she jumped onto one of the garbage bins and launched herself upward. Her hands gripped the top of the fence. She'd made it. She pulled herself up. Below her, a bright laser beam shone out and sizzled against the fence.

She dropped down into the street, but it was empty. Where were Erielle and the underworlders? Where was the car?

Then she saw two vehicle reverse lights heading her way. The car was traveling backward to reach her. Sayen raced up to the opening rear door and threw herself in headfirst. The car sped away, Sayen's feet in their oversized shoes hanging out the open door.

15

———

Makey's life hung in the balance over the next few hours. Erielle had transfused the artificial blood and carefully sutured closed the wound in his neck, but he didn't seem to get any better for a while. His pulse was weak, and he remained clammy and unconscious. Sayen, Jas, Carl, and Erielle took turns sitting by his bed so that someone would be there when—if—he woke up, or in case he got worse.

Sayen was asleep in the early hours of the morning when the news finally came. Carl shook her shoulder to wake her. "Makey?" she mumbled as she came to.

"Yeah. He's woken up. I think he's going to be okay. Do you want to come and see him?"

She sat up and pulled on her shirt and pants. She was in a sleeping bag in a communal bedroom. Underworlders lay around her in various states of sleep and wakefulness. She tiptoed out of the door that Carl had left open and went down one floor to the medical center.

The kid didn't look good. He was still as white as a ghost, and dark circles lay under his eyes. The wound on his neck was covered in a dressing, but angry red skin was visible at the edges, and fresh blood reddened the white gauze. Nevertheless, he managed to smile at Sayen as she went in. Erielle, Jas, and Carl were already there.

Makey's arms and hands lay listlessly on top of his bed coverings. He raised a finger. "Hi, Sayen. I guess I must look how you did when I first saw you aboard the *Galathea*, except you looked worse."

Realizing that he was reacting to her facial expression and was trying to calm her concern for him, she smiled in return—reassuringly, she hoped. "Yeah, well, you only have a scratch on your neck. I was nearly brain dead."

Her attempt at humor lightened the mood in the room a little. Jas and Carl chatted about what had happened in their failed attempt to capture a Shadow. Makey couldn't remember being shot, nor anything much after the shooting had started. No one was talking about what their next plan of action might be. It was enough for the moment that Makey hadn't died. Jas and Erielle seemed to have made their peace with each other.

The kid's eyes began to close, and Erielle suggested that they leave him alone to sleep and regain his strength. Carl volunteered to stay with him. As Sayen and the rest left, Erielle told Makey that he could drink some soup in the morning if he felt up to it.

She invited Sayen and Jas up to her room for a late supper or early breakfast, but Jas said that it had been a long night, and she would rather sleep. She left them on the second floor, and Erielle and Sayen continued up to the top of the building in a slightly awkward silence.

They went into Erielle's room, which was empty. Some dishes of food awaited them, along with a jug of some kind of home brew and beakers.

Erielle gestured for Sayen to sit down. She chose a cushion near the underworlder, across the table corner that separated them. Erielle's eyes were downcast as she ate.

After a while she said, "I didn't get a chance to thank you for what you did earlier. I was in too much of a hurry to get the blood into Makey."

"You don't have anything to thank me for," Sayen replied. "He's my friend. I was only doing what I could to help."

"If you hadn't been there, I don't think he would be alive now, and I would probably be in a holding cell."

"Like I said, I was just doing what I could."

Erielle lifted her dark brown eyes to Sayen's hazel ones. "I've gotta say, that's some modding you have. I've never seen anything like it."

"It isn't modding. My body's enhanced. We told you about the Shadows on our last prospecting mission, but we left out the fact that I nearly died. Jas saved my life, and she made them keep me in stasis until we got back to Earth. They couldn't revive me, so the doctors cloned my body and uploaded my mind into my new brain. Before they recreated my body, they offered me the option of choosing a few enhancements."

"Really?" Erielle's gaze lingered on Sayen's arms and chest. "Can you do anything else as well as you can run and jump?"

"I have super-sensitive vision and hearing, and my skin's extremely tough."

The underworlder reached out a hand, then hesitated, hovering over Sayen's bare forearm. "Can I?"

"Sure."

Erielle's fingers lightly stroked from her wrist to her elbow. A shiver ran up Sayen's spine.

"Strange," Erielle said. "It feels normal." Their eyes met for a moment. "But you're modded too, right?" Erielle asked. "You got the works at conception, didn't you?"

"You can tell?"

"Well, it's pretty obvious. You're flawless. Your face and body are completely symmetrical. The chances of being born looking so perfect naturally must be millions to one. And your intelligence is dialed right up too, isn't it? What's your speciality?"

"Math, I guess. I was a navigator. I *am* a navigator, I mean. When this mess is sorted out, I plan on returning to my job. Only this time I want to take advantage of my opportunities and not hide away from them. That's what I used to do, till I came close to dying. My parents were a little protective as I was growing up and—" She gasped.

"What's wrong?" Erielle asked.

"I forgot. My parents had me fitted with a tracker. I need to get it out in case the Shadows find out about it and use it to locate me."

"Your parents had a tracker put inside you? Wow. That's more than a little protective, I'd say, hun." Erielle frowned. "I might be able to get it out, but I'd have to operate on you in the medical center, and I don't want to move Makey. Things are still touch and go with him. If he's looking better tomorrow, I'll see what I can do then."

"Are you sure you can do it?"

"I used to be a doctor," Erielle said.

"You did?"

Smiling wryly so that her scar pulled her eye a little out of shape, Erielle said, "Is that really so hard to believe? I guess I don't look very professional anymore."

Sayen's gaze dropped to the underworlder's lean, bare

arms before returning to her face and its disfigurement. "What happened?"

"Did you think I was a natural? I guessed you did. After all, why would anyone choose to live like this? It's true, most of us underworlders are naturals, but not all. I was modded at conception like you. I was given my smarts with a stroke of a geneticist's gene splicer too. I don't think my parents' payment was in the same league as yours, but I did okay from it. Got into a good university, then medical school." She paused and laughed. "I don't know why I'm telling you this."

"Go on, I want to hear," said Sayen. Her privileged upbringing was rare, she knew. She'd always been curious about what regular lives were like, but it had always seemed crass and insensitive to ask.

Erielle sighed. "I went into cosmetic surgery." As Sayen raised her eyebrows, she touched her scar. "I know. Ironic, huh? Anyway, you wouldn't think there would be much call for facelifts and so on these days, but you'd be surprised. Modding produces beautiful children, but after they grow up they get older, just the same as people always have. Sure, there's plenty of aging treatments these days, but nothing as effective as the surgeon's scalpel."

Erielle's tone was quiet and intense. Sayen waited patiently to hear what she had to say next. As the underworlder spoke, she was breaking a piece of bread into tiny pieces.

"One day, I got asked to do some pro bono work. I agreed. My job paid well, and I had time on my hands to do a little good in the world. It wasn't until I saw my patient that I realized how much in need of good the world was." She took a deep breath and released it. "It was a little girl. She was badly disfigured. I thought she must have been in an accident. But my contact—I never met the girl's parents —my contact told me that she'd been born like that."

"How come?" Sayen asked. "Was she a natural?" She had heard about the many genetic abnormalities that modding had just about eradicated.

"No, she wasn't a natural. That was the point. It was all done very secretly. My contact brought the little girl in the evening and asked me not to put anything in the system about the operation. The nurse who assisted agreed to never tell anyone. I had to record the anesthetic and other resources as wastage to account for them. The poor girl looked terrible. I wanted to do all that I could to help her lead as normal a life as possible."

"Hold on," interjected Sayen. "You're sure she wasn't a natural? I mean...I don't get it."

"Sayen, my contact swore to me that the child's deformities were the result of modding gone wrong. He said that there were more like her, but the parents were bribed or threatened to silence. Their fee for the genetic modification was refunded, and they were offered a second treatment free of charge. And the babies with the abnormalities..." She swallowed. Her eyes were wet. "The babies were whisked away somewhere. I don't know where. The parents of the girl who was brought to me had insisted that they wanted to keep her. But they had to keep her hidden away. Our world barely tolerates people conceived naturally these days— people who look normal, let alone anyone who's different."

Lowering her fork to her plate, Sayen tried to take in what Erielle was telling her. "You're saying that sometimes the process goes wrong, but they can't tell until the baby's born?" A thought chilled her: what if she'd come out not quite right, after all the modding that her parents had paid for? Would they have abandoned her?

"It's one of the many sickening secrets of our world," said Erielle. "Just one of them. After that, I tried to continue working as normal, but I found I couldn't. I would look at my wealthy clients, who wanted a little fat removing here, a slight wrinkle smoothing out there, and I'd wonder if they'd given up a baby who'd failed to meet their expectations; if they'd returned a child who wasn't up to spec."

Sayen was suddenly not hungry. She pushed away her plate.

Silent tears rolled from Erielle's eyes.

"I'm sorry," Sayen said. She lifted a hand and slowly wiped away one of Erielle's tears with her thumb, brushing her scar. Erielle met her gaze. "How did you get this?" Sayen asked.

"Car accident. When you don't use autodrivers, they happen." She shrugged. "I could have fixed it up a little, but it seemed kinda hypocritical. I'd left my job by then. I just couldn't stomach it anymore. I couldn't stomach living in the sick, fake world we've created. I came here and joined the underworlders. They're my people now."

"And I guess I represent everything you underworlders hate?" Sayen asked.

Erielle smiled and wiped her eyes. "Yeah, you do. I'm sorry for being a misborn to you before. Try not to take it personally. After what you did for Makey, I know you're not like some digifreaks I've met."

"What am I like?"

For a long moment, Erielle didn't answer, and the silence stretched between the two women. Their eyes didn't leave each other's faces.

It was Erielle who made the first move. She leaned over the table. Sayen met Erielle's lips with her own.

Carl woke up. He was sitting in a chair, and his head and arms were on a bed. Disoriented for a moment, he sat bolt upright and looked around. As he realized where he was and remembered what had happened the previous day, he immediately swung around to Makey. The kid was motionless, and his skin was like alabaster. Carl leapt up and grabbed his shoulder.

"What?" exclaimed Makey, his eyes snapping open.

"Geez, I thought you were dead," said Carl.

"Ahhh," Makey said, wincing as he eased his shoulder from Carl's grasp, which made him move his neck. "No, I'm still around, thanks."

"Sorry. How are you feeling? Are you hungry? Or thirsty? Would you like me to get you something to drink?"

"Yeah, something to drink would be great."

Carl left him and ran up the stairs two at a time to Erielle's room to tell her the kid was awake again and needed her attention. He burst into the room without knocking. The underworlder was there and so was Sayen.

Erielle was looking out of the window and Sayen was lying on some cushions beneath a cover. The two had been talking when Carl interrupted them, though he hadn't caught the gist of the conversation. They both looked at him.

For a brief moment, Carl wondered what Sayen was doing there. Everyone else slept in one of the several communal rooms on the second floor. As the realization dawned, he said, "Oh, krat. Sorry," and he began to back out of the room.

"It's okay. What is it?" Erielle asked. "How's Makey?"

"He's woken up, and he's thirsty. I thought you'd want to know."

"I do. Thanks. Could you get him some water from the kitchen? I'll be down in a minute."

Carl ducked out and went to get the kid a drink. By the time he returned to the convalescent's room, Jas was there. She was talking to Makey.

"It's out of the question," she was saying. "Even if you were well enough, which you aren't, it'd be far too dangerous."

Makey said, "But—"

"Look, I overreacted in Antarctica," said Jas, "and I apologize for it. But the basic facts hold true. It was totally idiotic of me to allow you to come along on that trip yesterday. I should have made you get out of the car and picked you up later, no matter what Erielle had said." As Makey tried to voice further protests, she continued, "No. You aren't ready. But listen. I will train you, I promise. If we have the opportunity, I'll start as soon as I can. But we've got to make our next move, which is to capture a Shadow. For now, I'm *ordering* you to rest and get better. Are you going to follow my order or not?"

Makey glowered. "I'm going to follow your order," he said eventually, with an air of disappointment.

"Are we continuing with the plan?" Carl asked Jas as he handed Makey a beaker.

"I don't know what else we can do," she replied. "Erielle's right. Without proof, the Transgalactic Council have no reason to believe us. If these scanners that detect Shadows exist, we can show them that we've caught one, and they won't be able to deny that they're here on Earth. Under the Transgalactic Treaty, they'll have to help us."

"It's a shame that bugger Alef got away last night," Carl said.

"Yeah, it is. Shadow Alef, you mean."

"Yeah, Shadow Alef. You know they aren't the same as their victims, but that doesn't stop you from feeling like they are."

"Tell me about it."

Carl remembered the Shadow of the army officer Jas had killed on Dawn. He cringed. He seemed to be constantly putting his foot in it that morning.

The door opened, and Erielle and Sayen came in.

"How are you doing, kid?" Erielle asked.

"I'm feeling better by the minute," Makey replied. Some color had returned to his cheeks, and his eyes were brighter.

"Great." Erielle went to the door and bellowed, "Sark, soup," before shutting it. "If you're feeling up to it, I'd like to move you out for about an hour while I perform a small operation."

"An operation?" Jas asked. "Was someone injured in the raid last night?"

"No, we all got away unharmed, thanks to this woman," Erielle said, putting her arm around Sayen and giving her shoulder a squeeze. "But I want to do this operation as soon as I can."

"It's my tracer," Sayen explained. "She's going to take it out so we can destroy it."

"Of course. I'd forgotten," Jas said. "Are you sure you can do it safely?" she asked Erielle.

"Yes. I've extracted various pieces of shrapnel in this room over the years. I have everything I need." She turned to Sayen again. "I'll use a local anesthetic, okay?"

As Sayen nodded, Erielle's words reminded Carl of something that had long been bothering him about the underworlders. "So, you're happy to use modern technology?" he asked. "You said some of your people went to Dawn. I got to know those people and they wouldn't have anything to do with modern medicine or anything else that they thought was unnatural."

Erielle rolled her eyes. "Yeah, that's what they were like. We aren't all like that. They're confused, in my opinion. It isn't modern technology that we reject; it's what comes with it. The Government uses technology to watch and control you digifreaks. The only way to avoid it is to refuse to take part in normal society. You think we'd choose to live like this if we could have all the benefits you enjoy with none of the downsides? Of course not. That would be stupid. But if we have to give them up to be free, we will. Now, I don't suppose you know where that tracer is, Sayen?"

"I don't. I don't even have a scar. They must have had it added as my body was being grown."

Erielle grimaced. "That might make it harder to get out. Let me think. They would have put it in the safest place possible. It's probably somewhere without many nerves, and not very deep or near any organs. Ah, I have an idea. Turn around."

Sayen turned her back to Erielle, and the latter lifted her shirt and pushed her hands down the base of her back, under the waistband of her pants. Erielle frowned as she palpated the flesh at the top of Sayen's buttocks. Her face brightened. "I think I found it. Just here. Give me your hand." She took her hand and placed it on a certain spot. "What do you think? Can you feel it? I've got a scanner that should confirm it's there. I'll get it out."

"Great," Sayen said, "and then, can I finally get some clean clothes?"

Erielle laughed and nodded. Sayen prodded the spot on her buttocks. She noticed Carl and Jas watching. "Don't you two have something else to do?"

Sark came in with some soup for Makey, and Carl and Jas went to leave through the open door.

"Wait a minute," Erielle said. "Before you go, have you had any more thoughts on how to catch your Shadow?"

"I haven't," Jas replied. "Have you, Carl?" He shook his head.

"I heard that there's a security meeting tonight at the HQ," Erielle said. "A few Government officials are flying in from overseas. Would your Shadow usually attend those, Sayen?"

"Yes, he would," Sayen exclaimed.

"Tonight?" Jas said excitedly, but her face fell. "That place will be locked down after our attack last night."

"Maybe," said Erielle, "Or maybe they think you wouldn't dare attack them again so soon, especially when all you've got is a beat-up old car and a few weapons."

"Maybe they're right," Carl said.

"But if I were to help..."

"You're going to help us?" asked Jas.

"I'd like to lend a hand. And I've got quite a lot of equipment that should make things more interesting."

"That's great," said Jas. "What made you change your mind?"

Erielle shrugged. "I guess I finally understood this isn't a 'them and us' thing."

"I can't believe you lied to me about the invisibility spray," Jas said to Erielle.

"You think I'm going to tell a digifreak the truth?" the underworlder retorted as she retrieved the can from a cupboard in her munitions room. "This stuff's so precious, I could sell it and buy enough blackmarket food to keep the whole neighborhood fed for a year."

"I understand, I guess," Jas said. "Still, if we'd had it when we tried to catch the Shadow, maybe no one would have been hurt."

"I know. No need to remind me. That's one reason I'm coming with you tonight. If anyone's going to get hurt fighting these Shadows now, it should be me. I wasn't thinking straight, and Makey suffered for it. I should have sided with you when you didn't want to let him come with you, or I should have lent you the best equipment I had. I messed up, and the kid nearly died. I hope I'm going to put that right tonight."

"Don't blame yourself," said Jas. "If I hadn't been so hard on him in Antarctica, he mightn't have been so insistent. But neither of us knew what would happen, and he's going to be okay." Jas took the blaster that Erielle handed her and passed it to Carl, who inserted it in the holster inside his jacket. "How's Sayen doing?"

"She's got a sore butt, but she should be up and around tomorrow."

"Did it take you long to find the tracer?" Carl asked.

"No, but it had worked its way in a little, and I had to dig it out. I melted it in a burner. Sayen's got a few stitches. She wanted to come with us, the idiot. I told her to get some sleep, and in the morning I'd have a shadowy gift for her."

Jas was a little puzzled by Erielle's attitude toward Sayen. At first, she'd seemed to hate the ground the woman walked on. Then that morning she'd been overly familiar and intimate when she'd examined her, and Sayen hadn't seemed to mind. Now she was talking about giving her a gift. She wondered what was going on.

Tucking the blaster that Erielle handed her into the belt of her pants, she said, "How are we going to get there?" If they had to use the car that the underworlder had lent them the previous day, it wouldn't take the Shadows longer than a split second to recognize it. Or a split second longer to blow it to pieces.

"I've got a vehicle that'll help us blend in," Erielle said. "You'll see."

THEY WERE LEAVING the alley that led to Erielle's place. The underworlder had covered herself in invisibility spray, including goggles to cover her eyes, saying that she would explain on the way. Jas worried about what she might have in mind. The spray brought its own set of problems, though it gave them plenty of advantages.

Another large, black advantage was parked out in the street. A long, low Global Government limousine sat in the road, its doors open. An underworlder was giving it a final polish.

"Whoa," Jas said. "How the hell did you get it?"

"Now that would be telling." Erielle's voice came from Jas's right.

"What a beauty," breathed Carl. "Can I drive it, or is it autodrive?"

"They're either or," Erielle replied. "but I was hoping you would want to drive it. The autodrive safety control will stop us from getting too close to other vehicles, and that won't work for what I have in mind."

"And what do you have in mind?" Jas asked.

"I said I'll explain on the way."

Jas hated the last-minute planning, but Erielle had wanted to have someone survey the Security HQ and report back. They got into the car and headed out. Erielle sat in the rear and outlined how they were going to kidnap Sayen's Shadow.

Sayen had given them a detailed description of their target, but many personnel would be leaving the head-quarters that evening in Government cars, and they had to be sure that they had the right one. Erielle's plan was that she would slip inside and down into the car park, hope-fully undetected as she would be invisible. Her contact had scoped out the place, and she said she knew where to go for a close-up view of people entering the car park after the meeting. Carl and Jas would circle the block until Erielle notified them via short range radio that the Shadow was leaving, after which they would follow the car as it left the car park and make a second attempt at a kidnapping.

"I don't like the idea of you going in there," Jas said. "The place could be crawling with Shadows. Being invisible doesn't make you as undetectable as you might think. I found that out when we rescued Sayen. If it weren't for her and Carl, a Shadow Jas would be walking around right now."

"I'll be careful," Erielle said.

"How are you gonna get back?" Carl asked. "Even if we had time to pick you up, we can't see you."

"I can radio to tell you where to stop for me, and I'll do that if for some reason things don't work out. But you'll be busy catching your Shadow. I can make my own way home."

"I still don't like it," said Jas.

"Do you have a better plan?"

Jas was silent.

They dropped Erielle off a hundred meters or so from the Security HQ. It was weird seeing the car door open and close but no one apparently get out. They checked their radios were working, and set off to begin driving around the block while waiting for Erielle's heads up.

"I really don't like this," said Jas.

"You keep saying that," Carl said.

"I keep feeling it."

The radio crackled and fell silent. It seemed weird to be using such an old technology, but Erielle had assured them that it was *because* radios were such an old technology that they were the most secure comms the underworlders had.

Tension between Jas and Carl chilled the atmosphere inside the car. There was so much she wanted to say to him, but she never knew how to start, and the timing was never right. Something had nearly happened between them in

Australia, but now they seemed more distant than ever. Thinking back over the last few days and wondering why things were never easy between them, she realized that she hadn't been good company recently.

"Carl," she began before immediately drying up.

"Yeah?" His eyes left the road and flicked toward her for a moment.

"I...I'm sorry if I've been hard to get along with lately. It was going to Antarctica...it put me in a bad frame of mind. I've got some unhappy memories of my time there. I never thought I'd ever go back."

"No worries, Jas. Anything you wanna tell me about?"

"Not now. One day." Feeling a little better, she continued, "Hey, Sayen and Erielle have been acting a little weird toward each other. Is something going on between them, do you think?" she asked Carl.

"Yeah, of course. Can't you tell?"

"Oh yeah. Yeah, I thought so." In fact, Jas didn't find those kinds of things easy to notice. The added information drove her concern about what Erielle was doing a notch higher. If anything happened to the underworlder, Sayen would take it hard, and with her fears about her parents' safety, she had enough on her plate as it was.

A burst of static came from the radio. "I'm inside," said Erielle quietly. "Watching. Over." The radio was silent again.

Carl indicated and turned a corner. It was late evening, and the traffic was thin, which meant that they wouldn't be held up, but Jas worried that it also made their car noticeable and suspicious.

They'd passed the road leading to the car park once already. When they passed it again, a line of four limousines were queueing to get out. The meeting was over and the officials were leaving. Jas's heart pumped faster. It wouldn't be long now.

The radio gave a burst of static, then was silent. They drove the quiet streets for another turn. The suspense was agonizing. When would the kratting Shadow appear? Jas hated waiting. She itched to act.

"I think I can see him," came Erielle's soft voice over the radio. "He fits the description exactly."

Jas wished the underworlder wouldn't speak except when completely necessary. Though Erielle couldn't be seen, she could be heard.

"He's coming closer," continued Erielle. "I can see him better. Yes, I'm sure it's him."

Jas wanted to tell her to shut the krat up, but the sound of her own voice on the radio could also give the under-worlder away.

"He's leaving now. Get—"

Erielle's words were drowned out by an explosion of noise. Jas and Carl jumped in their seats and looked at each other. The radio went dead.

"What was that?" Carl asked.

"I don't know. I thought I recognized the noise, but—"

"Do you think she's okay?"

"I don't know. But we have to move. She said he's leaving."

"I know. We're nearly at the junction with the car park road. I'm slowing down. We should see his limo soon...Krat."

There it was: a limo waiting to join the main road. And right behind it was another one. Both had heavily tinted windows. Which one contained the Shadow?

Jas's mind was whirring as she tried to concentrate on the limousine in front of them. What had happened to Erielle? They'd received no further comms from her since that burst of loud noise over the radio. She thought of Sayen waiting for the underworlder back at the house. And she worried that they were following the wrong car.

She gripped her blaster. What if a human was inside the vehicle? They'd wanted to capture the Shadow alive, but if it died in the firefight, she wouldn't lose sleep over it. Killing an innocent person was another matter.

Carl seemed to be thinking the same thing. "Hey, look, we're coming up to a ditch on the side of the road there. What if I just force the car into it instead of you shooting the wheels out?"

"Good idea," Jas replied. She turned to scan behind them. The road was empty. No Shadows had noticed them this time, as far as she could tell.

Carl sped up. The limousine in front edged away. Jas wondered what the occupant was thinking. Had they noticed, or were they too occupied with an interface inside? Carl sped up some more, and moved out toward the center of the road, but the bright headlights of a truck appeared around a bend in front of them, and he had to move back into their lane.

Come on, thought Jas. The ditch was coming to an end. If they didn't manage to force the limousine into it soon, the opportunity would be lost, and she wasn't sure how they would stop the car without violence.

Carl hit the accelerator, and Jas's head whipped back. He zoomed out, but another truck appeared ahead. He slammed on the brakes and zipped back behind the limousine. The ditch on their left ended, and was replaced by forest. They were now way outside the city. They had to stop this car, and soon, before it reached its destination, where they might have to contend with other Shadows.

"Krat. I'm an idiot," exclaimed Carl. "It's so long since I've been driving cars, I forgot."

"What?" Jas asked.

Carl flipped a switch and pressed the accelerator. The pitch of the engine's whine rose, and the car sped up, but it also *flew* up. In a few moments they were above the car they were following. Carl flipped another switch, and the engine cut out. They fell, landing directly on the front of the limousine, which rolled to a halt, its autodrive safety system kicking in. Inertia carried their car forward, and they slid down onto the road.

Jas was out before the car stopped. She ran back to the limousine, her blaster in hand. The car's roof was dented, and she wondered if the damage was preventing the doors from opening, because the Shadow hadn't emerged and tried to escape. Carl was on the other side, holding his weapon. Their eyes met, and at a silently agreed moment, they pulled open the doors.

The occupant was sitting on Jas's side, looking more than a little surprised. It wasn't Sayen's Shadow. It was a woman with long, straight hair, wearing a kaftan.

18

———

They were nearly back at Erielle's place. A muffled thumping came from the trunk.

"Gee, I hope you're right," Jas said to Carl.

"I'm sure," Carl replied. "Well, pretty sure anyway."

Jas rolled her eyes.

"It has to be the Minister for Global Government Security," Carl said. "There can't be many women who wear kaftans to work at government headquarters."

"But is she a Shadow?"

"Sayen definitely seemed to think so."

Jas shook her head. If they were wrong, they were in deep, deep trouble. She wondered what the sentence was for kidnapping a Global Government minister. The courts would add assault to the charge, as they'd had to manhandle the woman to gag her and tie her up and lift her into the trunk. At least it was roomy and had plenty of air, and it was nighttime so the woman wouldn't get too hot. Still. They'd kidnapped a minister. She shook her head again.

When they arrived, an underworlder came out to meet

the car. Carl popped the trunk, and they went around the back to get the minister out. The woman's hair was all over the place, and her eyes were nearly popping from her head. A torrent of angry protests were muffled by the tape over her mouth.

"Better get her inside quick," Jas said to Carl.

She fought and struggled as he picked her up and hoisted her over his shoulder before carrying her down the alley. They thought it was safest to deposit the minister in the basement room where Erielle had put them before. They gave her a chair to sit on, but left her gagged and bound. The door had a secure lock.

Sayen was lying on her front in Erielle's treatment room. Makey was there, too. It was the early hours of the morning, and both were sound asleep. Jas gently woke Sayen and explained in whispers that they needed her to identify someone.

Wincing, Sayen eased herself off the bed and hobbled to the door. Jas and Carl went with her as she made her slow way down the stairs to the basement. Their victim had gotten out of her chair and wriggled over to the door, and they hit her on the head accidentally as they opened it. A muted cry of pain escaped her gag.

She didn't look any less furious than she had when they'd gotten her out of the trunk of the car. Her face was red and sweaty beneath her tangle of hair.

"Why did you take her?" Sayen asked. "Why didn't you kidnap Shadow Bernie?"

"Long story," Carl said. "But, is that the Minister for Global Government Security?"

"Yeah, that's her all right," Sayen said.

Jas exhaled in relief. "And you're sure she's a Shadow?"

"Well, I wouldn't go so far as to say I'm *sure*."

Jas groaned.

"She wasn't with Bernie when I was captured and taken away," said Sayen. "But she acted like a Shadow when she interviewed me, and it sure seems like there are a lot of them in that place."

The woman jerked and writhed on the floor, and tried to shout.

"Let's leave her to calm down a little," Jas said.

There didn't seem much point in replacing the woman in her chair, so they left her where she was after telling her they would be back in a little while. As they were climbing the stairs, Jas's hand froze on the rail as a realization popped into her mind.

"That noise," she said. "I know what it was."

"What noise?" asked Sayen.

"Erielle radioed us from the headquarters' car park, but there was a noise, and she was cut off."

"*What?*"

"What was it, Jas?" asked Carl.

"It sounded just like the burst of a fire extinguisher, which is strange...oh, krat."

"What, Jas?" Sayen asked urgently. "What is it?"

She hesitated a moment. She didn't want to put the thought in Sayen's mind, but now she couldn't refuse to explain. "Erielle was covered in invisibility spray, but she had to speak to tell us when your Shadow was leaving. If someone had overheard her, and wanted to find her..."

"They could spray the area with a fire extinguisher, and the foam would show where she was," finished Sayen.

"I might be totally wrong," Jas said. "I'm sorry."

They continued to climb the stairs. Sayen's head was bowed as she slowly took each step. When they reached the top, she turned a stricken face toward them. "Do you know when she's supposed to be back?"

"She'll be here by morning at the latest, I think," Carl replied. "She said she'd come back by herself."

It was going to be a long wait. Jas hoped with all her heart that the underworlder had made it out and was now on her way through the streets, invisible, returning to the home she'd created for herself and her people. If she didn't show up, they would have to find a way to rescue her.

Erielle had helped them. Without her, they would never have been able to capture the—probable—Shadow in the basement. She'd shown that underworlders and the rest of human society could and should work together to defeat their common enemy.

JAS'S STORY CONTINUES IN
BURNED

SHADOWS OF THE VOID BOOK 6

Sign up to my reader group for a free copy of *Starbound*, the Shadows of the Void prequel that tells the story of what happened to Jas Harrington in Antarctica, and for discounts on new releases, advanced reader opportunities and other interesting stuff:

https://jjgreenauthor.com/free-books/

(I won't send spam or pass on your details to a third party.)